FARAWAY

AN ESCAPE NOVEL

CASEY COX

PROLOGUE - EMRY

SIX YEARS EARLIER

Slam!

That'd be Jeremy Palmer's slimy palms slamming into my locker. I managed to catch a glimpse of his beady hazel eyes in the pocket mirror I had blu-tacked on the inside door of my locker just before he snapped it shut right in front of my face. A necessary hack to help with any last minute eyeliner adjustments—oh, and it helped with spotting incoming bullies, too. That part was, unfortunately, a daily occurrence.

At least it wasn't Connor O'Reilly's equally narrow but much more hate-filled eyes glaring back at me. That guy was positively evil. See, the good thing about having a serial truant as a bully meant that for a good chunk of any given term, he didn't show up at school half the time, leaving his four slack-jawed lackeys to do his dirty work on his behalf. They were stupid and mean, but at least they weren't Connor-level vicious.

"Well, lookie here," Jeremy snarled over his shoulder to his equally dumbass jock buddies—Ray Donovan, Sam Meyers, and Michael Cordon.

"He's wearing his favorite faggy Destiny's Child T-shirt."

I bit the inside of my cheek. *Urgh*, now was not the time to explain that it was in fact, a Pussycat Dolls limited edition Japanese tour merchandise vintage tee that I had draped over my gorgeously slender body. Jeremy and his goons wouldn't have appreciated the finer nuances of what any of that meant.

No one in Blessing, Texas would've for that matter. It might have been less than a hundred miles from Houston, but the only thing Blessing had going for it—or, more accurately, *through* it—was a train track tearing straight down the middle of the place, a shitty Main Street littered with what you'd expect to find in any shitty small town: a grocery store, post office, church, and diner. That was literally it. The train didn't even stop in Blessing. You had to go two towns over to get to the nearest station.

That proved, if nothing else did, that no one ever came to Blessing. People only ever left. People like me, one day very, *very* soon.

I suppressed a sigh as I turned around to face the meathead and his goons. I wondered what it would be today. I expected the usual mocking and teasing. That had sorta become second nature by this point. Some shoving? Pushing? Maybe. They never roughed me up too much, just enough to satisfy their pathetic little egos.

Calling me a fag? Hmm, strange how that wasn't the worst *F* word they could call me. And even stranger, I'd gotten so used to being called that—as well as *much* worse things—at home. With just a little over a month until graduation, I'd almost grown immune to all the taunts and teasing by this point.

Almost.

I wondered if they'd notice the pink bracelets that adorned my left wrist or the glittery pink laces I'd ordered on Amazon to level up my Nikes. But nope, apart from the T-shirt quip, so far, nothing else about my attire had drawn their attention. Maybe today they'd just stick to the usual routine of plain-out homophobia.

I didn't have to wait too long to be proved right. The gang started spewing out their tired, immature taunts, and I just stood there in my usual position: partly paralyzed with my eyes facing the ground. It felt like being under the shower with clothes on—wrong on so many different levels—but I was powerless to do anything. Respond, and I'd just be giving them ammunition. So I just stood there, getting drenched in their hatred.

As a swirl of "fags" and immature jibes whirred around me, I pressed my eyes shut, dreaming of a day where I could wear whatever I wanted, be whoever I wanted to be. That it wouldn't just have to be a hint of what I liked. That if I wanted to, I could stroll down the street wearing a goddamn kaftan just because I damn well felt like it. I knew that day would come, and with each dwindling day of the school calendar, it was getting closer and closer. I just had to hang in there for a little while longer.

Pink was my favorite thing ever—the color, the singer, and Princess Peach in Smash Bros, the game I'd been addicted to playing since I was a kid. She was my superhero. I loved the way she'd kick some serious ass while putting on such a submissive facade. What could I say? I related.

"You gonna say anything, fag?"

Uh-oh, it seemed that my silence was no longer good enough for Jeremy.

No, I liked my teeth just where they were—in my mouth. Though tempted, I kept that smartass crack locked in my throat. Still, I looked up at him. He raised one eyebrow slowly, deliberately, looking at me with a sly grin on his face. God, I hated him. Connor, the ringleader, I was petrified of, but Jeremy, he was just a douchebag.

"I hear it's hard to talk with your mouth full of dick."

That worldly observation came from Sam. He could always be counted on for bringing dicks to the forefront of any conversation. Funny thing, I mean, for a straight guy to be so phallically obsessed, right?

"I'm good," I replied, hoping it was enough to satisfy Jeremy. Without their leader Connor, these guys were a little lost. Still, you had to give them credit for keeping at it. Every morning before first period, at least a few lunchtimes each week as I made my way to the refuge of the library, and, if I wasn't quick enough, on the way to the bike stands before I pedaled my way from one hellhole to another.

"You got a boyfriend?" Ray asked with a sneer. His question drew snickers from the others for a reason I didn't understand.

"Nope." I shifted slightly and opened my locker, slowly starting to gather my things. They were stupid, but they weren't dumb enough to physically hurt me in the openness of the hallway. Too many witnesses and too many cell phones.

Still, I didn't want the conversation to veer into any territory that could lead to a threat of violence later on. Once you'd been subjected to bullying since—geez, let me think about it—first grade, you got a sense for how these things could quickly escalate. Sometimes, the lingering threat of future violence was the scariest thing of all.

It wasn't my fault I liked pink and had always been "expressive," as Mom called it, with my hands. And no, it wasn't that super clichéd thing of not liking myself and having to escape into a world of caricature—the super camp, stereotypical, effeminate gay guy. It was just me expressing a part of myself in a way that felt completely natural and right. For me, anyways. For my parents and almost everyone in Blessing, it was another matter entirely.

I didn't know what I'd do once I graduated. The plan started and ended with getting the fuck outta here. I had an uncle, a gay uncle, in Philadelphia. Dad didn't speak to him, of course, since he was a "disgrace to the family." Still, every year, Uncle Steve would send a Christmas card. And every year, Dad would refuse to even touch it and made Mom tear it up.

Last Christmas, I got up in the middle of the night and crept into the kitchen to pull the card out of the garbage. I stuck the two scraps of paper with his phone number together and added the number to my cell. Under a fake name, of course. I had enough money for a bus ticket and my uncle's phone number, so yeah, *that* was the be-all and end-all of my master plan.

I didn't care where I went, what I did, or where life took me. All I wanted was to get as far away as possible from here, this. And once I did, I swore to myself that I would never, ever, ever look back.

Drrrrriiiiiinnngg!

Ah, the first bell of the day. I let out a relieved breath as subtly as I could. The start of class would bring about an end to this round of bullying. I could see Jeremy creeping closer to me in the mirror. Once he got up into my space, real close, he eyed me up and down. He smelled like cheap deodorant and gross boy sweat. For a homophobic bully and all-round asshole, he sure did like spending time in my personal space. Not that I'd ever point that out to him. Got the feeling it wouldn't go down too well.

"See ya later, faggot." He tousled my hair, and with that, the three of them took off down the hallway, high-fiving each other like idiots for no reason other than the fact that they were idiots.

"Assholes," I muttered under my breath.

As I watched them in the mirror, tumbling down the hallway, one of them—Michael—looked back over his shoulder at me. He was the biggest one of the lot of them, but also the quietest. He hardly ever downright teased me. He just usually showed his agreement with chuckles and grunts. For just a split second, I caught a look of something in his eye. It might have been regret, a hint of something softer. I blinked and it was gone. So was he as the group disappeared around the corner.

I shrugged my shoulders out. Overall, that wasn't too bad. No direct physical contact, no threats of impending violence, just a few generic homophobic taunts. They didn't even call me girly or make fun of my appearance...too much. That felt like a small, pathetic victory of sorts.

But as I made my way to Mr. Perry's English class, a cold shiver tore through me. I shook—as in my body *actually* shivered before I reached the door. *What the hell was that?* I had no way of knowing it right there and then, but the next time I'd encounter my high school tormentors, it would change my life forever.

But it didn't happen that day. At least, it didn't happen at school. I survived the rest of the day without even seeing Jeremy, Ray, Sam, or Michael. Maybe they skipped school after first period? I had no idea, but there was no sign of them.

I should've been relieved, but it wasn't until I was on my bike, actually pedaling up my street, that I felt the tension leave me. Whatever had come over me before first period, that creepy feeling eased only a little. It stubbornly refused to leave me entirely.

No one was in when I got home. Dad worked at the meat

packing plant two towns over in Clemville, and on Thursdays, Mom would finish her shift at the post office and go visit Nana at the nursing home.

It was the only time I had the place all to myself. But after Mom walked in and found me trying on some of her makeup about a year ago, and Dad came home early after feeling sick and caught me jerking off in my room about three months ago, the allure of alone time in the house had lost its appeal.

Instead, I changed shirts, replacing the Pussycat Dolls with flannel—trust me, the symbolism of that pained me like you wouldn't believe—and headed out to Wilson's Diner, where my older brother, Will, worked.

Even though I hated home and school so much, they were still relatively protected environments. But out in town, that safety vanished. Most people kept to themselves, which was kinda strange for a small town, but there were a few outspoken people. Those who didn't look at me—they glared. Like my presence offended them, my very existence pulling some invisible trigger of all the things they hated.

So, yeah, when I left the house to wander into town, I butched things up. And if flannel had to be my armor, then so be it. It was only one more month, and then I'd burn every single piece of faux-straight clothing I owned. To me, fabric was just fabric, a color just a color. But not to the townsfolk around here.

I stepped into Wilson's and was greeted with a friendly wave by the owner, who also pulled server duties, Mrs. Cavelack. "Afternoon, Emry."

"Hey, Mrs. C."

"The usual?"

"Yes, please," I replied as I made my way over to the corner booth, my regular Thursday night hangout. It was out of the way and allowed me to while away some time. I'd wait for Will to finish his shift, keeping myself occupied with food and scrolling aimlessly on my phone. The place never got that busy, and Mrs. Cavelack didn't mind.

Will was six years older than me, and he started working here in his last year of high school. Normally, he'd babysit me on a Thursday night, but since he started working at the diner, my parents had asked Mrs. Cavelack if I could tag along. She'd never had any kids of her own, so she said she didn't mind.

I didn't need a babysitter now, of course, but it had become a bit like our weekly tradition. The walk home with Will was the only time the two of us hung out alone, and while he was kinda cool with the gay thing, he still struggled a bit with the gay *and femme* thing.

From his square jaw, deep voice, and lack of any ambition for getting out of this place, Will was about as small-town-straight as you could get. He'd just broken up with his high school sweetheart, Amanda Roberts. I didn't know what the deal was—he'd been his usual vague self about the whole thing—but a part of me held out hope that it freed him up to move to Philly with me, once I'd gotten myself set up there.

"Here you go, honey. Cheeseburger and onion rings." Mrs. Cavelack smiled warmly as she placed the food in front of me.

"Thank you," I said, lodging an onion ring into my mouth.

"I know you normally wait for Will, but we just heard the forecast on the radio. Seems like a storm's moving through. Gonna be a big one."

"Oh."

I looked at Will, collecting plates from a table at the other end of the diner. He looked up and gave a pensive nod. I guessed he knew what we were talking about.

"You're welcome to stay, of course," she went on. "But you might also wanna try to dash back home before it sets in."

"Okay. Thanks, Mrs. C."

It only took a couple of bites of my burger for me to settle on the second option. When it rained in Texas, it poured, and even though we only lived a ten-minute walk away, that was still enough time to get drenched to the bone.

I scarfed my food and ducked out of the diner just as the first heavy drops started to fall. I tugged at the sleeves on my flannel and took off briskly, hoping the gray clouds would hold until I got home.

Unfortunately, a little rain was going to be the least of my worries.

As I crossed the road, I spotted Michael Cordon walking toward me. Even though he was the least bulliest of the five guys, he was still a bully. My pulse ticked up a notch as we approached each other, both stopping at the same time on the deserted sidewalk.

"Hey," he said awkwardly and without any menace in his tone.

I was still on edge but managed to get out a relatively steady, "Hey" back.

He hooked his chin up, his dark curls falling away from his face as he took in the looming clouds overhead. "Looks like it's going to bucket down."

I didn't want him to see how nervous and fidgety I was, so I slammed my hands into my pockets. Most of it was due to the fact that I couldn't trust the guy, but a sick and twisted part of it was due to the fact that he was hot.

Yes, he was a little on the chubby side, but his face, my god. I kept a stash of *Vogues* and *GQs* under my bed, and seriously, the guy could've graced the pages in any of those magazines. Dark curly hair, broody deep eyes, and seriously full, luscious lips.

Argh, what the hell is wrong with me? Lusting after a bully. So, so wrong on so, *so* many levels.

Before either one of us could say another word, I spotted the ringleader and king of all assholes Connor's faded red pickup turning the corner and rearing up the street. My eyes widened, which made Michael look over his shoulder. "Fuck," I heard him curse. He turned back to me, his words falling out of him in a heated rush. "You have to go, Emry. Now."

His words were followed by a crack of thunder as the heavens opened up. "Go!" he cried.

For some reason, my feet remained cemented to the sidewalk. I didn't know if it was the rain, the sight of Connor's truck coming up the street, or the confusion that swirled in my mind about Michael. Was he trying to...protect me?

"Emry!" Michael grabbed my shoulders, giving me the shake I needed to wake the heck up.

I gazed into the blazing depths of his dark irises. My heart started clanging about my chest, completely irrationally. Was it his touch? Was it fear? I had no idea.

"You have to go, now," he repeated with a rising urgency in his voice. "Before he sees you. Turn around, take a left through Eighth, go down Mulberry, and cut through Ol' Man Jerry's farm."

Michael flicked his head back over his shoulder. A raindrop from his hair splashed across my cheek. He looked back at me. I was still partly frozen. I had no idea why. "I'll distract him. But you gotta go. Now, Emry... *Go! Run!*"

And with that, my brain and my legs clicked into gear. I turned around and ran as fast as my legs could carry me. The alarm in Michael's voice was justified, and he knew as well as I did that if Connor caught me out here, alone, it wouldn't end with a few jibes. It'd end with a fist in my face. Or worse.

I tore down Eighth and crossed over Mulberry Street as the rain got heavier. Our house was just on the other side of Ol' Man Jerry's farm, so it made sense to avoid roads and take the shortcut through the cleared-out field. The rain kept pouring down, so I was drenched either way. At least going through the paddock would eliminate any chance of Connor being able to tail me.

So I jumped the fence and ran, slowing down only a bit but still keeping a good pace. The rain blurred my vision and my lungs were pumping jagged breaths through my body as fast as they could.

Thunder cracked again, and then it happened.

A rod of lightning fell from the sky.

It was close.

Holy hell, it was close.

Fuck, it was coming straight for me!

I was about halfway through the field when I froze, blinded by the light and the realization that it was headed straight toward me. It was as if the lightning had been sent, directed, straight at me.

My eyes widened, and I threw my hands up to protect my face, but it was no use.

Milliseconds later, the glaring white light overtook everything I could see as it hit my body.

I, Emry Black, had been struck by lightning.

THURSDAY

1

EMRY

"I'm Hawk, this is Emry, and we're dick twins."

"Dick twins?" The cute jock startled for a moment, as his light brown eyes darted back and forth, looking at both of us like we were speaking a foreign language, like Canadian or something.

Hawk winked at me before turning his attention to the guy whose dazzling wide smile had captured our attention from the other side of the pool. "Yeah, dick twins," Hawk rumbled in that deep voice that we both knew—and had witnessed firsthand—was totally jock kryptonite.

I could see the guy's eyelids fluttering as the sound vibrated through his chest. Yep, we had him hooked. Now it was time to reel him in.

Hawk closed the space between the three of us, hooking a hand around my slim waist. "We might look a little different." That was putting it mildly. Hawk looked like he belonged on the cover of *Men's Fitness* with his six-foot-two frame of nothing but hard-earned muscle and natural sex appeal, while I looked like I belonged on the pages of *Vogue*, the genderfluid issue. "But I bet ya couldn't tell our dicks apart."

The jock's lips parted slightly. Yes, we were at an all-male luxury resort, and yes, it was clothing optional, so there were already plenty of dicks to look at, but something about saying those words in broad, late afternoon daylight ignited the air between the three of us with a sexual charge.

The guy settled back a little farther on his elbows, resting himself against the bar as he assessed the situation that had presented itself to him. The three of us were standing by the edge of the massive pool that was the heart and soul of the Elysian Resort, one of the most exclusive LGBTQIA+ resorts in the entire world. Hawk had spotted him first from the other side of the pool. We'd only arrived about an hour earlier, but as was our tradition, we flung our bags into our suite, stripped off, and headed for what would be our headquarters for the weekend: deck chairs by the pool.

Hawk and I had been coming to Elysian together for the last three years. And just to clarify, we were friends only. Friends who happened to have dicks that were carbon copies of each other: same length and girth, completely veinless. The only difference being that Hawk kept a tidy tuft of pubic hair on him, while I'd opted for the "smooth all over" look.

"I'm Brock, by the way."

Brock the jock. Nice. It always helped to remember names when rhyming was involved. We all smiled at each other but didn't shake hands. "Nice to meet you both."

"Same." It was the first word I said, and immediately, I scanned Brock's face for a reaction. My voice was high and a little feminine-sounding. Okay, *a lot* feminine-sounding. Would he hate it? Wince? Raise an eyebrow in disgust? Make up some bullshit excuse to go? Or just turn around and leave without saying anything? But, nope, so far it seemed I was in the clear.

There was a reason I let Hawk do the heavy lifting when it came to scoring us a hookup. He was masculine. Incredibly so. But it was as real and inherently a part of him as being feminine was true for me. There was no show to it. He wasn't straight-*acting*. He simply was who he was. It just so happened that who he was was accepted by a whole lot more people than who I was. You'd be surprised how many gay dudes weren't into femme guys. At all.

"So, are you guys a couple...in addition to being dick twins?" Brock asked as he flashed us another bright smile. The same kind that had pulled us into his orbit in the first place. His shoulders dropped and I sensed him easing into the situation and opening up to the idea of a threesome.

He was cute. Really cute. Short brown hair, sparkling and alive brown eyes, a bit of facial fuzz, tanned and fit as fuck.

Just *our* type.

"No, we're not a couple," Hawk said as he raised his arm, now draping his bicep around my shoulder. "We're just very good friends who enjoy playing together."

Hawk and I had met a few years back on a hookup app. We'd both been a little...creative in our profiles. Despite the fact we'd both presented ourselves as vers, the truth was we were both total tops. Let's just say that two tops did not make a bottom.

But Hawk had gone to all the effort of walking three hundred feet from his apartment to mine, and we were both horny as fuck, so we decided to fool around. And as soon as we unzipped, that's when we were both struck by the similarity of our cocks.

We exchanged pleasant blowjobs that evening, but the real score was making a new, good friend. Over the years, we'd grown even closer. He was now my closest friend, and we'd parlayed our identical dicks into a neat little threesome bait hook. Total win-win.

"I see." Brock took a sip of his drink before resting the almost empty glass by the edge of the pool.

I felt reassured by Hawk's touch, emboldened even. "Are you single?" I asked. I was more interested in letting Brock hear my voice than I was in his response, although, obviously, if he wasn't single or in an open relationship, this wouldn't be going any further. The only other person who despised cheating as much as I did was Hawk. The poor guy had been burned by a string of bad experiences.

"Yeah, I'm single," Brock answered, his eyes raking over me.

Okay, that time, he'd definitely heard my voice. And now he was appraising me. I tried my best not to stiffen under his gaze, steadying my breathing and keeping my face as neutral as possible. I didn't want to give away just how much scrutiny like this affected me, even if the guy wasn't really doing anything. It was me, my hang-ups, which normally, I was a boss at keeping locked away.

I loved the way I looked, but I knew it wasn't the conventional attractiveness that pulled guys toward Hawk like flies to honey. I was slender. I might have been nearing twenty-four, but I had a teenager's body. My dark blond hair took up a quarter of my face, always coiffed up and immaculate. I liked my hazel eyes, but I especially loved my thick eyebrows. They were a plucker's delight. Shaping them was one of my favorite things.

But most guys didn't see that. They looked at my scrawny shoulders or the lack of muscle on my arms. That, combined with the flamboyance of my hand movements, was a major turn-off. My ability to pick guys up and the past I had escaped from after graduation were my only two insecurities. In every other aspect of my life, I was smashing it—my career, my friends, my fabulous apartment that I had bought all by myself, my exquisite fashion sense. But yeah, despite all that, I still had two weaknesses that I did my very best to keep hidden out of view.

Good thing then that I had a good friend like Hawk to help me with the hooking-up thing.

And my past? Fuck my past. I never gave it a second thought, anyway.

Brock, however, skimmed over my body and brought his gaze to meet mine. "You've got gorgeous eyes," he remarked.

I swallowed, still a little unsure of how this was going to play out. "Thank you."

"But..." Brock leaned in closer toward us. My throat went dry. Great, this was the bit where he said he wasn't interested in *us*, but he really meant *me*. "I'm a greedy bottom. I don't like to share."

Hawk and I exchanged a knowing look. Mine had an air of relief attached to it as well.

"Brock." Hawk ran his hand over Brock's tightly drawn tricep. "You won't have to share. We're both tops."

The comment earned us a series of slow blinks, until the recognition settled. He looked at me. "You mean..." His voice trailed off.

Okay, so he'd need a nudge to actually get what we wanted him to understand about what we had going on here. "Total top," I confirmed as I dragged my tongue over my bottom lip.

A wicked smile stretched his lips as he moved closer and looped his smooth arms around our necks, bringing our foreheads so close they almost met in the middle "Well, then, boys, I think we might be in for a very fun afternoon."

The relief I had started to feel earlier was now met with a fierce desire. "There's only one thing I like more than one big dick," Brock informed us as he tightened his grip around our necks, the tips of our foreheads meeting softly. "And that's *two* big dicks."

Less than five minutes later, we were in Brock's bed, writhing around naked and kissing. Well, taking turns kissing him. The last scraps of any anxiety I might have been feeling were evaporating, giving way to a lustful longing.

But the thing about threesomes was that they could go either way. Even after passing the initial hurdle of finding a guy who was into both of us, the fact was that what guys often said they wanted didn't always marry up to reality.

In the three years Hawk and I had been hooking up with guys together, we'd seen guys who had told us they were size queens practically tremble in fear once they saw us naked and came face to face (or rather, face to cocks) with the enormity of the task at hand.

Other guys became shy, which was weird because it was often the guys that talked the dirtiest at the bar to us who, in the privacy of a hotel suite, flipped into lifeless starfish mode. That's why Hawk and I made a point to check in with the guy regularly, and if he wanted to stop or take a break at any point, we would respect that.

So far, Brock was showing no signs of being in over his head. "I want to see you two kiss each other while I suck you both off." If that remark was anything to go by, I'd say he was feeling just fine and dandy with everything.

As he dropped to his knees—his mouth replacing his hands at our cocks—it left Hawk and I staring at each other, slightly awkwardly. Of course, we'd kissed each other before. We'd gone down on each other, too. But whenever we did anything physical, it always felt a little...funny.

When we kissed—and it was always by request, never

something either one of us initiated—it was nice, but it wasn't that deep, passionate kind of kiss that you'd read about in romance novels. Where the world stopped spinning and everything else faded away as you got lost in a kiss that touched your soul.

No. The way Hawk and I kissed was more functional than anything else. It was like we were playing tennis and congratulating each other at the end of a series, or a game point, or whatever the hell the tennis term was for when the match finished.

Gay men and their ability to compartmentalize, right? And if I was good at one thing, it was being a master compartmentalizer... Hmm, that sounded like it could be the title of a cool quiz show. The Master Compartmentalizer...Before I could begin wondering what kind of game show it would be, I felt Hawk's fingers draped around my neck and he pulled me in for a kiss.

A deep, passionate kiss. Like the type you'd read about in romance novels, that made you feel tingly all over and sent a torrent of bliss surging through your body all the way down to your toes.

Wait, what?

I pulled away and shot Hawk a quizzical look. He scratched the back of his neck and shrugged his massive shoulders.

"You mffhhkph?" The sound of Brock's muffled words pulled my gaze downward toward him. He was trying to stuff both of our cocks into his mouth, so yeah, speech clarity wasn't going to happen.

He pulled our cocks out of his mouth and looked up at us both, his lips as swollen as Hawk's, and probably mine, after that hurricane of a kiss he'd just pulled me into.

"You guys okay?" Brock asked. The raspy undertone in his voice reminded me of what we had come here to do: him.

"We're good." Hawk raised his eyes back to me, waiting for me to respond.

"Yeah, all good here." I licked across my bottom lip and all I could taste was Hawk. I avoided his eyes, unable to meet the intensity behind them and instead focused back on Brock. "You like having two cocks in your mouth, Brock?"

His eyes lit up like fireballs. "Fuck, yeah. Your cocks are, like, heaven."

Brock wasn't the shy type or the guy who liked the fantasy of a threesome but was overwhelmed by the reality of it when presented with it. No. Brock was the third kind of guy—the one who fucking loved it and wanted to go wild with abandon.

My fingers smoothed over his jawline, and with Brock's pretty eyes still trained on me, I tipped my head to ask, "Well, then, wanna try two dicks in your ass?"

FRIDAY

2

MIGUEL

I loved Friday mornings. They were the last day of calm before the impending storm blew in. And by storm, I meant the surge of guests that would be arriving today and tomorrow. People from all over the world, from all walks of life, spending all or part of their vacation at the amazing Elysian resort, an LGBTQIA+ amusement park, sanctuary, and choose-your-own-adventure playground all rolled into one.

The housekeeping schedule was pretty relaxed for the day. That's why I only had half the team rostered on. It was good for them, a chance to get some rest and come back refreshed and fully charged for our Monday morning peak time.

As I stood in front of them, leading our daily 6:45 a.m. meeting, I felt proud of the team Leo, the owner of the resort, and I had assembled. Six sets of eyes were giving me their full and undivided attention, and I really appreciated it.

Sure, housekeeping wasn't glamorous work. But think about what would happen if hotels and resorts didn't have housekeeping. People often said one of the little luxuries of staying at nice places was experiencing a turndown service, or going out for the day to come back to a made-up bed and clean towels hanging in the bathroom. In our own small way, we helped to make an already special experience of staying at a luxury resort just that little bit extra nice.

But yes, it was background work that most guests, staying in most other resorts, took for granted until deciding whether tipping their housekeeper with a note was *too much*.

Not at Elysian, though. My crew here had the same respect afforded to them as other front-of-house staff—whether they worked the reception desk, served drinks at any of Elysian's five on-site bars, or entertained the crowd with their go-go dancing or DJ-ing skills. In Leo's book, all his staff were equal, and all of us were a tribe, a chosen family. Like the guests who stayed here, we came from all sorts of backgrounds, and some of us—like me—had all sorts of skeletons in our closets we were escaping from.

I scanned my to-go-over items for the day. I'd covered most of them. "Ah, team. Maintenance have asked if we could be a little more proactive in reporting any issues. So, if we're cleaning showers and we notice a drip, let them know, that sort of thing. It gives them a chance to get onto it before the problem gets any worse, and ideally, before a guest notices it and they have to report it."

Chase raised his hand. He was the newest member of our team and the most polite. He was also from Texas, like me. That part probably explained his good manners.

I shot him a warm smile. "You don't have to raise your hand, Chase, but go ahead."

"How would you like us to report it, Miguel? Do we add it to the repair log, or notify a maintenance person directly?"

He'd been reading the staff handbook, evident by the faces on the rest of the team members that were huddled in my small office. Marnus, Joel, Firass, Blake, and Noah stared at each other, then at me, blankly. It had been a while since they'd familiarized themselves with the handbook. Clearly.

"Yes, we have a staff handbook. Well pointed out, Chase." Not that we ever really used it. But the kid got points for attention to detail. "Just let someone from maintenance know about it."

Elysian was big enough that it felt like the proper, world-class, luxury resort that it was, but it still somehow managed to maintain a homey, comfortable feel, too. That was probably down to Leo Carter. He ran this place like it meant the world to him. Because it did.

"One last thing, team. We have Jack and Ari staying in Suite 401. They got in late last night." Jack and Ari were two of Leo's oldest friends and regulars at the resort since it opened in the late '90s. They flew down from New York at least bimonthly and were known well and loved by all the staff.

Ari had recently gone through chemotherapy to treat a particularly aggressive strain of prostate cancer. This was their first trip back. Jack had emailed me earlier in the week, requesting some discretion. As a result of the cancer, Ari was experiencing incontinence issues, which were understandably embarrassing for the guy.

I saw Chase's face. Now he was the one with the blank expression. "They're regulars," Marnus explained to him. "They're in their sixties, but they're the funniest guys ever. They love getting dressed up for all the theme parties and they are so super friendly and approachable."

"That's right," I took over. "And while they're staying here with us this time, I will be attending to their room. I've made a note of that on all your room schedules, and I'll be reminding all team members about it tomorrow as well."

I could see a couple of guys wanted to ask a follow-up question, but no one actually did. I decided to move on.

"We've got a full house this weekend, guys." I rallied the team. "So we're going to need to be on it. I want us all pulling together, working fast and efficiently. But not at the expense of detail, okay? Guests pay a lot of money to stay here. They are entitled to have expectations and to have those expectations...exceeded."

I looked around my office and was met with a sea of nodding heads. I didn't need to be telling the guys any of this. They were all as hardworking and dedicated to doing a good job as I was. But a little reminder never hurt, either. Especially since these days, people took to social media and review sites to complain about the smallest details. We needed to be on top of everything.

"Any questions before we get started for the day?" I asked.

When no one said anything, the guys got up, stacked the chairs one by one into the little nook at the back of the room, and filed out. I smiled at each of them as they left. Leading a team of guys who were my age or older could have been fraught with problems, but thankfully, this was a dream team to manage.

Not that becoming head of housekeeping had even been in my sights when I arrived penniless at Elysian over five years ago begging for work. Leo took pity on me and let me help out with some odd jobs that needed to be done.

I dove headfirst into it all. No job was too dirty, too disgusting, or too beneath me. Clearing out blocked toilets, laundering soiled linens, mopping away vomit—I did it all. Happily. Hoping that in some small way, it would act as a penance, a way of alleviating the guilt I'd felt ever since graduating high school.

You see, I'd been a bully. What was worse was that I'd gotten away with it.

Until one stormy night when everything changed...

I left home soon after graduation, not to college but back to my parents' country of birth: El Salvador. It was an unmitigated disaster, nothing like how I'd imagined it in my head.

So when I arrived at Elysian after having begged every other gay resort in Florida for any spot of work they could throw my way, I wasn't just broke—I was broken.

Leo gave me a shot. And to this day, he says it was one of the best chances he ever took. I didn't know about that. I came here as a form of self-punishment, not to get rewarded with promotion after promotion. But that's exactly what happened.

I worked my ass off, sixteen hours a day, six days a week, doing anything and everything around the resort. And I was good at what I did. So good that Leo picked up on it and, in a very short space of time, I went from having a job that had no title other than *unofficial shitkicker* to housekeeper, then housekeeper/front of house, then deputy housekeeper, until I ended up leading the whole department four months ago when Tony Williams retired.

Was this what I wanted to be doing for the rest of my life? Probably not. Had I sacrificed my dream to settle for this? Probably yeah.

As my unexpected career that should have been a punishment advanced, I took to chastening myself in another way: suppressing a lifelong dream. Because bad people didn't deserve to have good things happen to them.

I switched on my computer, and as I waited for it to boot up, I leaned back in my chair, swiveling from side to side. For as long as I could remember, I was obsessed with comedy. Mom and Dad would watch a lot of sitcoms. As immigrants, it was another way for them to learn and improve their English. Reruns of *Friends*, *Seinfeld*, and *Frasier* were always bouncing off the walls in the living room. And amongst the canned laughter and often predictable situations that I only paid vague attention to, I discovered small threads of poignant humor and emotion cutting through.

Like the *Friends* Thanksgiving episode where each of the characters revealed their worst Thanksgiving memory. Or that time that George's mother caught him masturbating in *Seinfeld*. Something about those little nuggets of humor tinged with reality jumped off the screen and into my brain and made me think, *That's what I want to do one day.* Create *that*. Make other people feel *that*.

I'd never done anything about it, though. Part self-inflicted punishment, but mainly due to the realization that I most likely didn't actually have any comedic talent. Although, I was on the verge of changing all of that.

And soon. Like, tonight soon.

"Hey, got a sec?" Leo's muscular frame filled up the entire door frame to my office.

"Of course." I gestured to the empty chair at my desk. "Come in."

Leo sat down and we went through the rosters for the next week. He also checked in to see how Chase was fitting in with the team. All standard stuff, but I knew the guy well enough to know that he didn't come in here to talk about work. Something else was on his mind, and it didn't take long for the real purpose of his visit to come out.

"So." He steepled his fingers as a grin stretched his lips. "How are you feeling about tonight?"

Ah, I should've known. In addition to being an all-round nice guy, Leo was also the biggest support system a person could ever hope for. If he heard about a dream you had or an opportunity you wanted to pursue, Leo was the type of guy that would find a way to make it happen for you.

In this case, he'd organized a stand-up comedy night at the resort. Ostensibly, it was a way to entertain guests. But we had nightly go-go shows and weekly karaoke nights for that. No, this wasn't just an innocent little comedy night. This was an open mic night where anyone could perform.

And somehow, by pure coincidence, my name had found its way onto the signup sheet. All the more intriguing was how my name happened to match Leo's penmanship so precisely. But yeah, that was the kind of man he was. Despite my initial reservations, I was beyond grateful he'd gone to all this trouble for me.

"I'm feeling..." Hmm, was there a word for feeling shit scared before taking that first awkward baby step toward fulfilling the biggest dream you've ever had in your life? Because whatever that word was, I was feeling it. Big time.

Instead of saying that, though, and sounding like a crazy person, I settled on, "I'm feeling okay."

A gentleness simmered in Leo's eyes. "It's normal to feel a little nervous, Miguel."

"I know. But I'm pretty well prepared."

"You are." Leo reached across the desk and patted my hand. "I've heard your routine. It's good. Very good. You have nothing to worry about, my friend."

I had run through my act with Leo yesterday. He laughed in all the right places and it seemed genuine. I knew he'd hate telling me if I stank, but he'd also be kind enough to not let me get up on stage and make a complete fool out of myself in front of a crowd. So I knew that what I had was at least good...ish.

My comedy was in the vein of something between Ellen and Tina Fey. Smart, witty, and observational, without being too mean or cruel. I'd done enough of *mean* and *cruel* in high school to last me a lifetime. Although I had to admit that a part of me was drawn to the comedy stylings of people like Joan Rivers and Margaret Cho.

"What are you thinking, Miguel?"

Leo was an astute guy, so there was no way of keeping anything from him. I decided to lay it all out on the table.

Inhaling sharply, I asked, "What if I stink?"

"Then you'll fucking stink," he replied matter-of-factly, before throwing in his customary, "if you'll excuse my French."

The speediness of his response surprised me. "Stinking is a bad thing, Leo."

"It is, Miguel. And yes, it will sting a little. But this is your first time. Don't aim for being the best stand-up comedian ever in the history of comedy. Go for giving it your best shot. And then the next time you do it, you'll be better. And you'll keep getting better the more you do it."

I exhaled as I absorbed his baby steps approach. He was right, as usual. Ellen and Tina Fey were pros with years of experience under their comedic belts. As long as I didn't completely crash and burn, I'd be happy with that.

Leo got up to leave. "Oh, and listen. Jack called me last night. He told me he's spoken with you about Ari's condition and that you've offered to personally assist them during their stay."

I nodded, not sure where he was heading with this. "Uh-huh."

Leo leaned against the doorframe and clutched his fingers over the center of his chest. "Thank you, Miguel. That's so nice of you. You really are the best." He shot me an appreciative smile.

My lips tightened. No, I really wasn't.

I was the worst.

3

EMRY

"Oooh, *honnayyy*." I kissed my lips toward the mirror as I took an admiring glance at my reflection. Hair on point, styled up with a gentle wave to the right. Eyebrows *gorgggg*, plucked to within an inch of their lives but on standby and at the ready to craft my face into whatever emotion I was feeling. (That was the whole point of eyebrows, right? I mean, if eyes were the windows to the soul, then eyebrows were the doorway to sass and gags, right?) And my lips, sparkling and bedazzling and just made for kissing.

I lifted my chin and applied the last layer of foundation over the top part of my neck just one last time. A tiny line creased the middle of my perfectly smooth forehead. Truth be told, I didn't really like makeup. Hair styling and lip gloss were fine, fun even. But the foundation? Especially in a place like Florida? Urgh, a nightmare.

But still, people would take one look at me and think, *Of course a guy like that would wear makeup* and never, *Hmmm, I wonder if that guy wears makeup to cover the marks that won't heal because his father spent years beating, choking, and throttling him.* It was easier to let people believe it was option A and not the sad truth of option B.

But life was too short to look back and be bitter, and as I used to like to joke, *I* was too short to be bitter. And hey, I loved my five-foot-six frame—it was a great excuse to find shoes with a heel!

My phone lit up with a text message. I picked it up from the bathroom vanity top. It was Hawk. He'd found us a place. And by *a place*, I meant deckchairs by the pool in prime viewing position. I flicked him back a quick response saying I'd be down in a few minutes.

I smiled, thinking about just how much a creature of habit Hawk was. He always insisted we arrive on a Thursday, whereas most guests only started streaming in on a Saturday. He said he liked a day or two to settle in and get a feel for things.

And by *a feel for things*, he meant getting a fuck or two under his belt. Not that I minded. Our work schedules back home in

Philadelphia were crazy. Hawk worked in construction. He had a full-time job working for a good friend and was trying to start his own plumbing business on the side. Meanwhile, my work took me out of the country for at least half the year. So, between the two of us, getting away to Elysian a couple of times each year was our chance to unwind, relax, and gorge on hot man meat... Together, of course.

With one last glance in the mirror, I gave a satisfied nod and headed to the wardrobe. Don't worry, I wasn't one of those people that took forever to decide what to wear. That was part of the appeal of staying at a clothing-optional resort. Less was definitely more—and I had no problem flaunting the more that I was blessed to have been endowed with.

I draped my self-made, purple and black sequined kaftan, a gorgeous piece that not even the most progressive European fashion designers could manage. I had to make it on my own. *Story of my life.* Good thing I was a whiz on a sewing machine and not afraid of a hot glue gun, either.

I stepped out into the kitchen and living area. Hawk and I always stayed in the same suite, 707. Hawk liked it for a number of reasons: it was on the ground floor, it was close to the pool, it was even closer to the gym (where he spent at least two hours every morning, while I vigilantly maintained my beauty sleep regimen), and it had two separate rooms, each with an en suite bathroom. The perfect blend of privacy and accessibility.

I grabbed my matching clutch. Okay, *clutch* might not have been the right word. It was a purse. Wait, you got me. It was a bag, but guuurl, not just any bag: a custom-made Mansur Gavriel Zip Bucket Bag. The bag was iconic enough on its own, a modern marvel right up there with, I don't know, how Kim Kardashian's ass managed to stay attached to her body. But after running into one of the lead designers of the company after she saw me performing on the European leg of my tour, I was gifted this gorgeous purple and black, pebble-grained, faux leather stunner.

That was one of the downsides of hanging out in a clothing optional resort. Not wearing pants meant no pockets. And no pockets created a problem. Where was the modern gay man supposed to store all of the essential items he needed? You know, like a phone, wallet, room key, condoms, lube, cock ring, makeup, water, breath mints, backup cock ring, a book, and coconut-oil-infused sunscreen. Total first-world problems, but, like...real.

I created a cloud of Issey Miyake in front of me, stepped through it, and headed straight for a deckchair with my name on it.

"Well, hello." Hawk lifted his sunglasses and shot me an admiring smile...as well as a slow up, down, and all around look.

"You like?" I shifted faux modestly on my legs to give the impression of being a shy schoolkid.

"I do, indeed."

I placed my bag by the side of the deckchair and began to arrange the towel. Hawk was already in position, which meant lying down. His muscular frame was sprawled over every inch of his deckchair. Oh, and he was completely and totally naked.

The pool area was surprisingly busy, maybe about a quarter full. Slightly strange given how early it still was, but since it was a Friday morning, all the other guys here were early birds like us. A dedicated breed. First to arrive, last to leave. And horny as fuck to boot.

I sighed a little despondently. Hawk picked up on it straight away. He always gave the impression of being so aloof, the strong and silent type, but he was so attuned to me, always noticing even the slightest change in my demeanor.

"What's wrong?" He'd placed his sunglasses back down over his eyes, but I could see his jaw clenched with worry.

"I'm happy to go naked. It's just...well, this thing isn't going to be seen by anyone." I gave a twirl and the light fabric of my kaftan lifted into the air around me.

Hawk got up and pulled me in nice and close to him, his

massive hand gripping the small of my back. "Good thing you look beautiful either way, then."

"Oh, you think so, huh?" I flung my arms over his wide shoulders.

Don't worry, we weren't flirting, just putting on a show. I could already feel the eyes of guys on us. This was our little warmup act, letting out the universal gay scent of *we're up for it*.

Hawk pulled me in even closer, and before I knew it, his lips were brushing against mine. Whoa...okay, *that* wasn't part of the usual routine. It was a soft kiss, but enough for me to register the taste of coffee on his lips.

I pulled back a little. "You okay?" I asked, lifting one of my perfectly manicured eyebrows.

"Yeah, fine." Hawk shuffled back to his deckchair and lay down. "Just happy to be here and..." His voice trailed off, before he squared his shoulders and looked up at me. "I've missed you. It's been a good few months since we've seen each other."

"I know, I know. My bad." I shrugged out of my kaftan, draped it over the empty chair next to me, and joined Hawk, settling in on the deckchair beside him. "I only got back from Vienna on Monday."

"How was it?"

I rested my head against the pillow attached to the backrest of the lounge. "Amazing. Things are going so well. It was my most successful tour to date."

"I am so happy for you, Emry."

I was happy for me, too. The last thing I'd expected when I got hit by lightning was to wake up and be able to play the piano perfectly, much less to end up touring the world and playing in some of the biggest concert halls in Europe.

It made zero sense. I'd never played piano in my life, not a single lesson growing up. And it's not like we just had a piano lying around the house. I didn't even have the slightest interest in music. Fashion, yes, but music was meh to me.

The doctors explained that it was neurological. My brain got rewired, and somehow, I got access to things I didn't even know existed, like classical music.

I took a sip of water and turned to Hawk. "How about you? How's work going?"

He grumbled but was cracking a small smile at the same time, too. "Busy."

I nodded. It was his default response. And I got it. Working full-time and trying to get a side hustle off the ground was hard work and very time-consuming. "But you're enjoying it, right?"

"I am. Or, at least, I will be. Soon, I hope. Ask me again in six months."

"I'll ask you plenty of times before then," I quipped as we both settled in and scanned the scene in front of us.

"So..." I finally spoke after a few minutes of silence. "What's the plan for today?" I pretty much knew the answer, but I liked the familiarity of hearing him say it anyway.

"Poolside hangs, a fuck, some lunch, chillin', and then a comedy show."

A fit of giggles bubbled out of me. I loved how Hawk used words. He was direct and straight to the point. There was never any chance of not knowing what the big guy meant. It was one of the things I loved most about our friendship. We'd never had any silly miscommunications or stupid fights, and believe me, for two gay dudes, that was a super rare achievement.

"You happy with that, Emry?" He cracked a smile as he peered up at me from under his sunglasses.

"Yep." I smiled back. "Actually, wait. What comedy show are you talking about?"

"They're having an open mic comedy night here at the resort."

"Oh, they've never done that before," I remarked.

Hawk nodded. "First time. Leo came up with the idea. It's actually a really sweet story. He's got a staff member who's always wanted to try his hand at comedy, but never has."

"So, Leo's organizing a chance for him to pursue his dream?" My hand was clutched over my heart, touched by the sweetness of the gesture.

"You got it," Hawk confirmed.

"I love Leo so much. He's the best guy in the world."

"He is. I just wish..." Hawk looked away.

After a few beats, I prodded. "You just wish what?"

Hawk's jaw bunched up. "He's so busy looking out for everyone else. I just wish the guy would spend some time on himself, you know? It's been five years since Dante died and I know he's still not over it."

"It takes time, Hawk. And it wasn't just how he died. It's what happened afterward."

Hawk had been friends with Leo for way longer than me, but he had introduced me to him at our first stay here and we'd all become friends ever since. I'd only heard about what had happened to Leo's partner, Dante, through Hawk. Leo never spoke about it at all.

"The comedy show sounds like fun," I said in an attempt to lighten the mood.

"Yeah, it will be." The hitch in Hawk's jawline eased. After a few beats, I saw his lips twitching. I recognized that movement. He was getting horny. Hawk grabbed my hand and gave it a tight squeeze. "You up for some dick twin fun, Emry?"

"Sure," I replied breezily. "I'm up for another round. Or two."

4

MIGUEL

So far, the morning was busy but running smoothly. Marnus had called in a faulty stovetop in one of the oceanfront suites to the maintenance crew, and Chase asked about the possibility of offering a pair of guests a late checkout since their flight wasn't until 10 p.m. that night. I informed him of the resort's policy that we couldn't extend checkout times Friday through to Sunday, but that guests were welcome to stow their luggage at reception and could still make use of the resort's facilities until they needed to leave.

I finished off the last email I was working on and noticed the time in the corner of my laptop screen. It was just before ten. I got up from my desk and headed over to pay a visit to some special guests.

A few minutes later, I was met with two beaming faces. "Miguel!" Jack cried out, flinging his arms around me, followed shortly by Ari. Yep, even though they were guests, by now, they felt like so much more than that.

"Come in, come in." Jack gestured for me to follow them into their presidential suite. As I followed them into the living room, I took some time to assess Ari. He seemed thinner, and his face was gaunt, but overall, the guy seemed to be looking well. Or at least as well as could be expected.

"Would you like some tea or coffee?" Ari offered, but I shook my head.

"Thank you, but no. I'm on the clock, and you know the boss. He's a slave driver."

"He's the worst," Jack concurred, and we fell into a light laugh.

As silence returned to the room, Ari dropped his head as Jack took his hand. "Thank you for doing this, Miguel." His voice was soft and I could tell he was feeling embarrassed.

"No need to thank me. I—"

"Yes, there is," Ari insisted. "This is so way below your pay level, and I—we—both really appreciate it."

I waved my hand dismissively. "Guys, really, there's no need."

And then I paused for comedic effect. "My pay level really isn't that great to begin with."

The three of us laughed again, and I let out a breath I'd been holding in since stepping into their suite. This was my favorite part of my job, and of working at Elysian—making a genuine connection with people and being able to help them out.

"So, let's go over how we can make this work for you..."

As we worked out the finer details of our arrangement and I noted what they requested, I could see both of them relaxing a bit. Yes, it wasn't fun to have to request a special housekeeping service, but it wasn't Ari's fault he had survived cancer and his body was still dealing with some of the aftermath of that horrific experience.

Trust me, in housekeeping, you saw it all, and you either became immune to it, or you couldn't hack it and left. We're kinda like medical professionals in that way. This was not a career for the squeamish.

Once we'd settled on a plan that worked for everyone, I was just about to leave, when Jack asked me, "So, how are you feeling about the show tonight?"

The question caught me a little off guard. I'd been so focused on them and their needs that the show had been the last thing on my mind.

"Uh, good. I think. I'm looking forward to it."

"Well, we'll be there in the front row, cheering you on," Ari added, raising a triumphant fist into the air.

I knew they were only trying to encourage me by showing their support, but it suddenly brought home the all too real fact that there would be an audience at the show. Of people. Real people. Not the imaginary laughter track I crafted in my head whenever I had been rehearsing, or writing, or planning my act.

I felt a tightness in my chest but did my best to ignore it as I got to the door. Ari remained on the couch, while Jack escorted me out. As he held the door open for me, he followed me outside and leaned in to speak. "Seriously, thank you for doing this, Miguel. I've been trying so hard to be strong and keep myself together for Ari, but I am exhausted."

"I know you are. And you've been doing a terrific job. But while you've been looking after Ari, who's been looking after you? Carers need a break, too," I pointed out. "There's absolutely nothing wrong with that. You're here to enjoy yourself as well."

Tears welled in Jack's eyes as he listened to me. "You have no idea how much it means to hear you say that, Miguel. I've been feeling so guilty. He's the one going through the cancer. I have no right to make it about me."

"Hey." I gave his forearm a gentle press. "Self-care is nothing to feel guilty about. You're not being self-indulgent by looking after yourself. You need to do what you need to do to be strong yourself, so that you can be strong for him."

"Thanks, Miguel. You're a decent man." We hugged and I left, but Jack's words wouldn't stop buzzing around in my brain.

I wasn't a decent man. And I was starting to realize that it didn't matter how much time passed or how much I tried to inflict punishment and misery on myself. This gross guilty feeling that I carried inside of me was lodged in there permanently. Maybe that was the biggest punishment of all?

I'd made other people's lives hell in high school, and now, I was doomed to make myself feel like shit for...how long? There was never any excuse that justified being a bully, but in my incredibly meek defense, it was a case of eat or get eaten. As a slightly chubby kid of immigrant parents in small-town Texas of all places, my whole life was about fitting in. Of being the one to be on the offense so that I'd never be backed into a corner and forced to be defensive.

Making my way back to my office, I walked down a fragrant cobblestone pathway filled with sweet-smelling gardenias, jasmine, and hibiscus blooming in vivid shades of red, white, orange, and violet. My mind drifted to my mom. She loved hibiscus flowers. And I knew that she and Dad only wanted what was best for me, but denying my heritage, changing our names to sound more

American, removing any traces of where they had come from, it was all too much. Yes, it came from a goodhearted place, but ultimately, it was nothing more than a misguided attempt to fit in.

It screwed me up as a kid in high school. Worse, its effects lingered to this very day. And all of that effort to look, be, sound, and feel like an American, *like we belonged*, was all for nothing. I didn't grow up and go off to college to pursue a law or medical degree like my parents wanted. My parents—as they frequently reminded me—sacrificed everything so that I could pursue a good life and fulfill all of my dreams. Little did they know that *their* dream had become *my* living nightmare.

After graduation, I left town and was totally lost, adrift in a sea of emotions that were pulling me in myriad different directions. Should I go back and reacquaint myself with my lost heritage, or should I move forward and be grateful to live in one of the richest, most advanced countries on the planet?

Or should I spend the rest of my life suffering the consequences of what happened on that dark, stormy night one month before graduation?

Yeah, *that*.

It always came back to what I did to Emry Black. The poor kid. And no matter how much time passed, I would never, ever let myself forget it.

5

EMRY

Sex should never be a United Nations-level negotiation, but when you're femme, unfortunately, it often is.

Denver—yes, that was his actual name; Hawk had double-checked—was perched on the edge of my deckchair. He was gloriously built, a tall tower of lean muscle, topped off with an angular face and thick mop of dark curls. He'd strolled past us a few times, each time slowing down and craning his neck to get a view of us in our full, resplendent, naked glory.

Well, a view of Hawk, at least. Me, he didn't look twice at me. But after his third walk-by and before his fourth, Hawk managed to convince me that he'd be able to get the guy interested in both of us.

It sounded pathetic, that he'd have to resort to convincing me he could convince a guy to have sex with both of us, but it was also an all too common occurrence. Even though my kaftan was now neatly folded away in my custom-made bag, even the sight of my slender, naked body screamed *Camp As Fuck*. Or it could have been the gold bracelets that dangled off my wrist or the sparkling purple nail polish shimmering on the tips of my fingers. Regardless, whatever Denver saw when he looked at me, it was clear he wasn't digging it.

"So, you two are a package deal?"

The disappointment in Denver's voice stung. Not only me, it hurt Hawk, too. I could see it in the slight shifts in his demeanor, how his face tightened and in the way he drew his legs in closer to his body. What had started off as light and fun flirting between the two of them was slowly deteriorating the more Denver's lack of attraction to me became obvious.

"Because, you know"—Denver leaned in closer to Hawk, grazing his fingers against the ridge of his tricep—"I do some of my best work one on one." He tried whispering those last three words into Hawk's ear, but Hawk pulled away from the guy.

"We're a team." Hawk was in full-on defensive mode now, and I had a feeling we wouldn't be doing any dick twinning with this guy. "Both of us, or none of us."

Denver pulled back and directed a scathing sneer at me. "If I wanted to get fucked by a woman, I'd buy my best friend, Tessa, a strap on. I mean, no offense, dude."

Oh, right. Of course. How silly would *I* be to get offended by a comment like that?

"I don't think this is going to work out, Denver." Hawk's jawline was clenched so tight I could picture his teeth bursting through any second now.

Denver's eyes drew into narrow slits as he tilted his head back toward Hawk. "You sure about that, big guy? I can definitely make it worth your while." Before Hawk could respond with what I was pretty sure was going to be a big fat no, Denver added, "I'll even let your friend here sit in the corner and he can, you know, watch and finger himself or whatever."

You could have heard the air being vacuumed from around us as Hawk got up and gave Denver a hearty slap right between his shoulder blades. "I think we're good. Enjoy the rest of your stay here, Denver."

His words might have sounded nice, but the grumble beneath each and every one of them was unmissable. Denver's shock at getting rejected was quickly replaced by spite, as he stood up and shot us both an evil glare. "Fine, whatever." He turned back to Hawk, sneering at him as he eyed him up and down one last time. "You're not that hot anyway."

I could see Hawk's fists balled up, his knuckles white, and I knew it was taking every ounce of his willpower to keep his cool. Thankfully, he managed to bite his tongue as we watched Denver saunter off to the other side of the pool.

But all of Hawk's seething rage evaporated into thin air as he slid back into his chair and looked across at me, softness crinkling the corners of his eyes. "Are you okay? I'm so sorry about that douchebag."

"It's not your fault." I was still spinning in shock. You'd think that after getting rejected as many times as I had—just for being who I was—I'd have gotten used to it by now. But no, it still hurt. Every single time.

Denver might have been a grade A dick, but it could've been worse. My biggest fear was walking into a room and someone seeing me and bursting out laughing. Yep, that's happened. Luckily, only a few times, but trust me, it's the most paralyzing, soul crushing feeling in the world.

Compassion filled his eyes as Hawk ran his hand gently along my arm. "I think you're beautiful and wonderful and amazing."

I appreciated Hawk's kind words and gave my best attempt at a smile. "You know, if I'm holding you back, you can just go ahead on your own. I don't think I'm in the mood anymore. I can just chill here. I'm reading a great book at the moment."

"No." Hawk's voice was firm, defiant.

"Hawk." I sent him a knowing look. "I don't want this to be an issue for you. It's my thing to deal with. Not yours."

"And what might that *thing* be?"

My head bounced against the soft pillow at the back of the deckchair as I groaned. "We both know it. I'm too femme for most gay guys."

"Brock didn't seem to mind yesterday," Hawk pointed out.

"True." I nodded. "But he's the exception, not the rule. Apparently, most guys—guys like Denver—just see me as a woman with a strap on."

"Not most guys, just one asshole."

I met Hawk's determined gaze. "We need a drink," he announced. "What would you like?"

"Vodka soda, please."

"Stay here." Hawk shot up onto his feet. "I'll be right back."

As I watched him make his way over to the bar, I couldn't help but notice the way guys were responding to him. With smiles, with appreciative glances up and down the length of his toned and tanned body, even with the occasional cheeky back slap. I couldn't blame them. Hawk was one seriously hot slab of man meat.

I never got that reaction from guys. Occasionally, I got some props and positive remarks when I dressed up in one of my fierce outfits. Guys were happy to cheer me on and look at me, but never fuck me, it seemed. And it sucked. People had so many misconceptions about femme guys that they just stuck onto me, too. And all of them were bullshit.

The biggest one of all was that I wanted to be a woman. Nothing could have been further from the truth. One of my closest friends back in Philly, Kayla, was trans, so I had a small glimpse of what that world entailed. And I was not trans. As much as I adored women, that's not who I was or wanted to be.

For me, it was about expressing myself. It just so happened that the way I expressed myself was largely wrapped up in the label of femme. Yes, I liked the color pink because it was bright and made me feel happy. Yes, I talked with my hands and flailed them about as if I didn't have any bones in my fingers, but I couldn't help it that I got excited. Yes, I liked fashion and creating my own amazing clothes, but I only did it because men's fashion was so restrictive and boring. Khaki shorts? Puh-lease. As if you'd ever catch me in a pair of those.

But I was also the captain of the Philadelphia paintball team until my work schedule got so crazy and I wasn't in town that much anymore. I loved putting on the camo gear and helmet, nursing a fake gun in my hands and tearing about the course and splattering opponents with pellets of paint. It got me buzzing with excitement, and yes, some rage steamed out of me, too. Naturally, I followed a grueling session up with a two hour mani/pedi/facial/massage at Philly's finest day spa.

Why couldn't I have it all? Be who I wanted to be? And if that made other people uncomfortable, that was on them. After the shitty start I got in life, didn't I deserve a chance to live out my dreams in my own way?

I wasn't asking for a lot. I just wanted to be myself. Why was that so hard for so many people to accept?

6

MIGUEL

"How do you feel?" Marnus asked me as I paced up and down in the dimly lit backstage area.

Normally, there'd be go-go dancers scurrying about back here, or a local band Leo would sometimes book, or jittery karaoke-rs deciding on what level of embarrassment they were willing to subject themselves to. But tonight, it was just a bunch of first time wannabe comics, and you could cut the tension with a knife.

"I'm so nervous I can't tell if I want to throw up or wet myself," I groaned.

Marnus chuckled. "That's good. You're being funny. That means you're in the right headspace. You are going to kill this, especially with your new and improved routine."

Ah, yes. About that. The reason for me not knowing which of my bodily functions I was about to lose control over first.

Marnus and I had clocked off at our usual 4 p.m. finish time, but instead of heading home to prepare, I'd taken him up on his offer to hang out in the staff headquarters. I'd brought in a spare change of clothes with me since I had a feeling one of the guys would invariably ask me to stay.

Marnus asked how I was feeling and I told him about the routine I had planned. I was met with a disconcerting look. He didn't think it would fly. According to him, my nice routine that I had prepared and run over with Leo yesterday wasn't what people wanted. Nice was dull and boring and something that belonged to another era, like the 2010s. I hated to say it, but I thought he might have had a somewhat valid point.

Objectively, my act was all right. Passable. Good, not great, but hopefully enough to at least draw a few laughs from the audience and not get booed off stage. But was that what I wanted? To play it safe? I honestly didn't know. I was torn.

So, hastily, and with the help of Marnus, Joel, and Pierce, I put together an alternative routine. Meaner, edgier and, according to all the guys, totally *ROTFL*-worthy. Whatever the hell that meant.

So now I had a decision to make: did I play it safe and go with the nice routine, or did I take a big risk and switch to the edgier, meaner act? More risk meant potentially more of a payoff...or it could just all blow up in my face. There was that, too. I really didn't know which way to go here.

"Are you sure about this?" I asked him for the fifty-seventh time as the MC made his way past us and onto the stage. "I'm having doubts."

"Yes, I am sure." Marnus placed his hand on my shoulder. I assumed this was his way of trying to make me feel better, but for some reason, it only weighed me down even more. "No one likes nice stuff anymore," he insisted. "Just look at Ellen."

"Hey." I turned to face him with a scowl. "I like Ellen."

"Yeah, but she's old news. And ironically, it's because people uncovered that she was mean. If she was upfront about it, people would've eaten it up. But she was dishonest about it."

I wasn't sure I was following Marnus' logic. Sounds of the audience applauding and laughing at the MC's intro jokes filled my eardrums. Shit, I was the first act, and I still didn't know which of my two routines I'd be performing in, oh, about sixty seconds.

I glanced over at Marnus' grinning face and furled my eyebrows. "I mean, should I really be taking advice about what's hot and relevant from someone who looked into his closet and decided *that* top was the best thing he could wear tonight?"

Marnus threw his head back and let out a loud snort. "Yes, that's exactly it, Miguel. Comedic gold. That's why your mean-boy routine is going to slice, dish, filet, and slay the competition." He threw in a few theatrical hand flurries to accentuate his words.

I tapped my fingers against the top of the pile of cue cards I was holding, growing less and less convinced by the second. "Yeah, but a joke like that is between us. You know I'm not some mean, heartless monster. I'm just harmlessly teasing a friend. Whereas some of the material I've got here"—I flung the cards between us—"some of this is really harsh."

"People love harsh." Magnus wrapped his fingers around my

shoulders as he started gently shoving me toward the stage. The announcer had already started to introduce me. "If you're lucky, someone in the audience will record it and you never know, it could go viral."

"I feel like I'm about to be viral...as in sick," I said flatly, but it only drew another laugh out of Marnus. "Are you sure it's not offensive?"

"Positive."

I heard the announcer call out my name.

"You'll be fine," Marnus said from behind. "Now, go!"

And now, with a not-so-gentle shove, I was on.

I didn't know how I was walking, but somehow, my feet carried me to the bright spotlight in the center of the stage as applause and cries of my name—which sounded suspiciously like Leo's deep voice—bellowed out from the darkened audience in front of me. I grabbed the mic stand and adjusted the height of the microphone so it was closer to my mouth.

Here went nothing...just, you know, my lifelong dream.

I inhaled a deep breath, slapped on a smile, and opened my big, fat, stupid mouth...

7

EMRY

A comedy show was just what I needed to get my mind off that asshole, Denver, from earlier that day. Despite doing my best to shake it off, I couldn't help but let it affect me. Hawk was brilliant, as always, checking in with me during our delicious lunch at Elysian's Michelin-rated restaurant, as well as for the rest of the afternoon, too. He even offered to skip his afternoon gym session to stay with me, which was a super big deal. No matter how much the guy worked, he always managed to fit in not one but two gym sessions. Every. Single. Day.

I appreciated his concern, I really did. I knew how super lucky I was to have a good friend like him. Unfortunately—and completely unintentionally—it only served to remind me over and over again of what had happened.

Assholes like that were the reason why I removed all hookup apps from my phone and my life. If people could be cruel to my face, what happened online was a thousand times worse.

But it was Friday night, we were on a weekend vacation, and I was determined not to let that jerk eat into another minute of my thoughts.

We were hanging out with Leo and a bunch of other staff near the front of the stage. The place was packed and buzzing with anticipation. I'd never actually been to a stand-up night before, so I was looking forward to it.

"Are you okay?" Hawk asked me for what must've been the gazillionth time that day. I guess I had broken off from the main group conversation and gone a little quiet.

"Fine," I said, taking a sip of my drink. "I was just thinking about how I've never actually seen live comedy before."

"Yeah, Joel was just saying the same thing." Leo must have overheard us and chipped in, tipping his head toward one of his staff members. Hawk, Leo, and I hung out when we'd been down here, but it was the first time we were hanging out with other resort staff, too. They all seemed like nice guys. There was Joel, Pierce, and a guy named Marnus, but he wasn't around at the moment.

The MC was wrapping up his introductory speech just as Marnus joined us. He seemed a little out of breath, but excited. "Okay, it's done," he announced to the other guys.

Leo raised an eyebrow suspiciously. "What's done?"

"I got him to change his routine."

Hawk and I looked at each other, puzzled. "I have no idea what they're talking about," I mentioned to him.

"Neither do I."

Marnus filled us in. "Miguel was going to do a plain old boring routine. Nice for the '90s and for anyone old enough to remember the original versions of *Full House* and *Saved by the Bell*, but it wouldn't stack up today. So, the guys and I managed to talk him out of it. He's going to perform something...edgier."

Leo folded his arms across his chest. "How edgy?"

"Oh, you'll see. Right about...now."

Applause rang out in the air as I spotted the man of the hour. I'd never met Miguel, but geez, if comedy never worked out for the guy, he should definitely consider modeling. He was giving off major Ricky Martin *"Livin' La Vida Loca"* vibes, except his hair was wavier, his lips fuller, and his eyes broodier. Way, way broodier.

As he approached center stage, I picked up on a certain nervous energy, too. Leo had mentioned this was his first time ever attempting this, so it made sense the guy would be anxious. I closed my eyes and sent him some good vibes. I was used to performing in front of crowds now, but when I first started my career, I'd be throwing up backstage with the worst stage fright. It was an awful thing to experience, kinda like motion sickness but you weren't actually moving.

Miguel tapped on the microphone and let out a shaky, "Hey, it's great to be here tonight."

I settled in on my stool, prepared to laugh my ass off. I mean, even if he wasn't hilarious, he could still do with the support. Besides, how bad could it be?

We were all about to find out.

"My name is Miguel, and this is my first time doing anything like this. Which, funnily enough, is what your dad whispered into my ear last night."

Like I said, I'd never seen live comedy before, but I assumed that the natural order of things went *comedian says joke, audience starts laughing*. That hadn't happened with this one, but hey, it was just his first attempt. It would surely pick up from here.

"I'm the head of housekeeping here at Elysian—"

That elicited a few cheers from our group.

"Thank you. My parents are from El Salvador, so in a way, I shouldn't be surprised I ended up in this line of work. I guess my first clue should've been when my first words weren't *mamma* or *pappa* but"—he tapped on the mic to make it sound like someone knocking on a door—"*housekeeping*."

That drew a couple of chuckles from the crowd, but more coughing than anything else, it seemed. I glanced over at Hawk, who looked back at me and shrugged. Something was feeling very, very off about this routine.

"I've been in housekeeping for over five years now," Miguel marched on, talking through the crack that underpinned his voice. "So, if anyone wants to find out how to get the slut out of Egyptian cotton, I'm your guy."

More coughing, accompanied by a few groans. I could have been mistaken, but I was pretty sure I heard a faint *boo* in there, too.

"What the hell is he doing?" Leo directed his line of fire at Marnus, who looked just as shell-shocked as the rest of us.

"Uh, I don't know. It sounded much funnier this afternoon."

"Shit," Leo muttered under his breath. "This isn't good." He turned to Hawk and me and explained, "Miguel is the nicest, sweetest guy you'd ever meet. I have no idea what he's doing, but this isn't him, you guys."

Hawk and I nodded politely. What else could we do?

"But I did go to college." I had to give Miguel props for continuing and not giving up, but he was starting to look more flustered with each passing moment. "And I had a major. Major depression."

If this was a late night TV show, the band member would have hit the drums to make that cringey *ba-dum-tss* sound. Miguel wasn't that lucky. He was met with stifled silence.

"Can you do anything, Leo?" Hawk asked.

Leo was looking pissed. "Like what? He's clearly received some bad advice and is doing the wrong routine." He glowered at Marnus and the others when he said it. "If he'd stuck with the original plan, we wouldn't be in this mess right now."

Marnus stepped in and offered, "Look, it could be worse. At least he's not doing the bit about menstruation."

And right on cue, Miguel asked the audience, "Do we have any ladies in the house?"

A few hands were raised and a muted "Yeah" could be heard.

"So," Miguel went on, unclipping the mic from the stand and walking toward the left side of the stage, "can someone please tell me, what is the deal with periods—"

Before he could answer his own question, a sharp series of boos filled the air. In a way, I was actually relieved. We'd been spared. I had a feeling the joke wouldn't have ended well.

As the cries and now heckling got louder and louder, Miguel—to his credit?—kept talking through it. It was getting harder and harder to hear him, though.

"Get him off."

"Boo!"

Leo craned his head. I could see a vein threatening to burst at his temple. He was positively fuming. His eyes managed to find the MC who was standing by the other side of the stage from us and he seemed to speak without talking, just gesturing. The message was clear—cut Miguel off. Pronto!

The MC stumbled onto the stage, as if Leo was standing

behind him and had pushed him onto it, just as Miguel was valiantly finishing off a non-menstruation joke. "I was so ugly that when I was born, the doctor took one look at me, before his eyes widened in horror and he screamed at my mom, 'Save yourself. *Go. Run!*'"

A couple of things happened right at that very moment. The MC snatched the microphone away from Miguel, setting off one of those uncomfortable, super high-pitched mic sounds. It cut Miguel off instantly, which was probably for his own good. The booing and calls for Miguel to leave (I might have been omitting a few of the audience's more choice words) only grew louder as he slumped his way off the stage.

But I didn't see or hear any of *that* chaos because the glass I had been holding slipped from my fingers, dropped to the floor, and shattered into a thousand tiny shards.

Memory was a funny thing. And those last two words that Miguel had uttered triggered me and took me back to a time and a place I had been spending my entire adult life trying to get as far away from as possible.

"Are you all right, Emry?"

I heard Hawk asking me the question, but it came out all distorted and echoey. My vision was graying at the edges. I was standing, but I couldn't feel my body.

I was frozen.

My feet couldn't move. Heck, I couldn't even turn my face to look at Hawk. I'd been stunned. And it wasn't because of the atrocious act we'd all been subjected to.

I would've recognized that cry of "*Go. Run!*" anywhere. They were the last words a certain someone had yelled at me that night I got struck by lightning a month before graduation.

I knew the guys referred to him as Miguel, but whoever had just slunk off the stage wasn't Miguel.

I knew it made absolutely zero sense, but I was more certain of it than anything.

That guy wasn't Miguel. It was Michael Cordon: my high school bully.

8

MIGUEL

It probably defied every law of physics, but somehow, the booing and angry cries sounded louder as I sped up and ran the last few steps off the stage.

There was blowing it, and then there was blowing it on a magnitude of *fucked-up-ness* that was out of this world. And that was precisely what I had done.

I was angry at myself and mortified, but more than anything else, I was left with this feeling of looking/feeling/being so stupid... How could I have just gone out there and done *that?* My heart was pounding so hard I thought I'd throw up. Thankfully, I managed to get off the stage without adding that disgrace as the final bit of my routine.

The people that were swarming around backstage parted like the Red Sea in front of me. They'd seen it. Of course they'd seen it. Everyone had. The guests and, oh my god, Leo, Jack, Ari, and all the other staff. I stomped over to a small table that had a bunch of water bottles on it, grabbed one, and drained it. Then another. I was gulping down my third bottle when I felt a strong hand pressing softly against my shoulder.

I recognized the touch, as much as I didn't want to. I closed my eyes as I spun around slowly. When I dared to peek them open, I wasn't met with anger, or hostility, or anything that I completely and totally deserved. Instead, I was met with two kind eyes that felt like they weren't judging me. They were feeling my pain.

I fell into Leo's arms and began sobbing. Hey, I had literally zero dignity left. Why not add public crying to the mix? Leo held me for as long as I needed it, gently running his hand up and down my back. Once we pulled apart, he walked me over to a quiet corner of the room.

"How are you feeling?"

"Like complete and utter shit." I finished wiping the tears off my face, before adding, "I am so sorry, Leo. I fucked up. Big time. *Huge* time."

"Hey, hey, hey."

I knew he wanted me to look at him, but how could I? The man had taken a chance on a kid he didn't know five years ago and given him a job. He was the best boss a person could hope for. He'd become a close personal friend over the years. He'd organized this entire night for me and this was how I repaid him after everything he'd done. How could I ever look at the guy again?

"Granted, Miguel, that wasn't your finest hour. You made a mistake. But you'll learn from it. You can't beat yourself up over this."

"That's where you're wrong, Leo. I can and I will."

He didn't know it. No one did, but I had years of practice beating myself up over the mistakes I'd been making my whole damn life. This would just be another thing to add to the growing list of things to punish myself for.

At that moment, I noticed some movement behind Leo. Marnus' face popped up over Leo's shoulder, his lips drawn into a thin line.

"I'm sorry," he pleaded with a pained look on his face that probably came close to matching mine. "This is all my fault, Miguel. I shouldn't have talked you into it."

"*We* shouldn't have talked you into it," Pierce added. Joel was there, too, as well as some other people who remained shadowy background figures in the dimly lit room.

"No, guys. There's only one person to blame for this fiasco fuckery, and that's me."

"But we talked you into it," Joel protested.

"Yeah, but I'm a grown-ass man who could've told you to stick it where the sun don't shine. I made the choice. I changed my routine. I wrote the damn thing. Those were my words. My jokes...if you can call them that. I appreciate what you're trying to do, but this is all on me, you guys."

Leo, being the voice of reason as always, stepped in and suggested, "Let's go back to the staff bungalow. I'd suggest having a few drinks here, but we might be safer out of public view."

I actually managed to smile and I heard some of the others chuckling at his comment.

"We'll have a few drinks together, commiserate, and then wake up tomorrow and put this all behind us."

He made it sound so easy. This was meant to be my big night, my chance to fulfill a lifelong dream. And now, it had been dumped onto a *let's leave this behind and never speak of it again* pile. My dream was in tatters, and I had no one to blame but my own stupid self.

The guys turned and started leaving, while I was still steadying myself. As much as I appreciated Leo's sentiment, this wasn't something I'd be able to drop and forget about tomorrow. If anything, I was now more confused than ever.

What did this mean? Was my dream over before it had really begun? Did I really have no comedic talent or was my mistake choosing the mean routine over the nice one? Or was I just an asshole who deserved to be stuck in housekeeping for the rest of his life?

As I composed myself a little and slowly made my way, following the others, a figure stepped out of the darkness in front of me and stopped me in my tracks. I looked up and into a set of strangely familiar hazel eyes. And just when I thought this night couldn't get any weirder, the guy who was standing in front of me said one word that made my blood freeze.

"Michael?"

9
___

EMRY

The guy looked like he'd seen a ghost. His eyes, his lips, his eyebrows—everything on his face that could move went in every direction it could possibly go in, leaving him looking completely and utterly horrified.

I mean yes, he'd just been booed off stage, but it wasn't that.

It was me.

He just stood there, not saying a word. The guy didn't seem capable of responding, just blinking hard and fast as if he was hoping to blink the sight of me away. That was all I got from him, but a response that involved actual words? That would be a hard no.

"Are you Michael?" I repeated, in case somehow he'd missed it the first time. "Michael Cordon."

Just as his lips parted, Leo's voice boomed from behind me. "Is everything okay here?"

"Uh, yeah, we're fine." He finally found his voice. "You guys go ahead. I'll catch up in a bit."

Leo didn't say anything, but I could hear the sounds of footsteps fading behind me. But once he was gone, the guy in front of me went back into deep freeze mode.

My teeth burrowed into my lower lip. This situation called for a change in approach. Instead of asking him who he was—which was clearly stumping him for some reason—I'd tell him who I was. "I'm Emry. Emry Black. I grew up in Blessing, Texas. I went to Tideshaven High School."

We said the name of our former school together.

I snapped my fingers, like a scientist making a major breakthrough. "So it is you?"

His first words back to me were not what I was expecting at all.

"I thought—I thought you were dead."

"Dead?" I scrunched my face, confused. "Why would you think I was dead?"

His eyes shifted from side to side as he came in closer to me. He dipped his head, his voice barely more than a whisper. "You got hit by lightning, dude. That night, when I sent you out into the field. After you got hit, we never saw or heard about you ag—"

"Stop." I raised my hand between us, before pinching it against the bridge of my nose. "I don't want to talk about that."

The memories of that night had no place in my life. I never let them rear their ugly heads and I had no intention of starting now. I'd spent too much time trying to forget. I didn't want this Miguel-slash-Michael guy taking me back there, reminding me.

"As you can see"—I cleared my throat, collecting my composure—"I'm not dead."

He cocked his head to the side and for the first time since I'd approached him, he looked at me. Properly. The way someone stared intently at an abstract piece of art trying to get a handle on it.

I noticed how dark his eyes were. If I thought they were broody from where I was standing in the audience, being so close to them was another thing entirely. They were like magnets. I was watching him watching me, and all I could feel was a surge of electricity between us that was like nothing I'd ever felt before. And I'd been struck by lightning.

The longer he stared at me, the more convinced I became that he was in fact, Michael Cordon. It had to be. His voice was the same and his gorgeous, model-esque face had matured into an even sexier version of his boyhood self, but the rest of him? Boy oh boy, what a transformation. In high school, he'd been a little on the chunky side, which I always thought was hot, actually. Not enough for it to be a big deal, but noticeable. He hung out with his bully buddies so he was automatically immune to any teasing himself, but he'd clearly focused on his body since graduating.

Standing in front of me, he wore all black, and his body looked like it had been chiseled out of marble. He wasn't big or bulky but instead, perfectly proportioned. Ridges of muscles traced down his upper arms, his shoulders tapered into a slim waist, and his legs, despite being clad in dark slacks...well, let's just say it looked like he wasn't the kinda guy who skipped leg day at the gym.

I opened my mouth to say something else to break the silent spell that we had fallen into, but my lips tripped over the fact that my brain hadn't come up with any words, other than to call him Miguel and stop referring to him as just "the guy." That was what he called himself after all, so I wanted to respect that.

The still silence between us carried so much pent-up energy, and I became conscious of how long it had been since one of us had said anything. I couldn't even remember who had spoken last or what part of this unexpected reunion we were up to. What was meant to happen next? Was there a protocol or etiquette for running into one of your high school bullies after he'd just crashed and burned the fuck out of what was meant to be a comedy show? I had a feeling there was no *For Dummies* guidebook for navigating this situation.

My emotions hadn't even had a chance to catch up to this, much less begin processing any of it. What were the correct or appropriate things to be feeling when you stood face to face with your former bully? Although to be fair, Michael—I mean, Miguel—had been the nicest of the gang of five that tormented me and tried to squeeze the femme-ness and gay-ness out of me.

In a way, he'd not only saved me from the bully that probably would've beaten me up that stormy night—he'd saved my life. If I hadn't run out into that field, I wouldn't have been living the life I was today.

Weird, then, that he thought he had killed me. But I guess, looking back on it, I did leave town pretty much straight after. And I'd never looked back. Not even once. Not until, well, right now. Huh.

He shot me a questioning glance. "I—I don't even know how to begin to process this."

"Fair enough." I was more than a little lost myself.

"I just think I need to get insanely drunk." He scratched his cheek. "Come back to staff headquarters with me."

I couldn't tell if it was a question, or a request, or something in between. He shot me a smile, a pained one, and it only confused me even more. Then I remembered. His routine. The one he'd bombed at. Oh, wow, and now, me dropping another bomb on him. Okay, I could totally see how that was a lot for one person to deal with.

He gestured toward the door, and I followed him as we walked out of the backstage area. My mind was racing at a million miles an hour. I still couldn't believe I had run into him...of all people...of all the places in the world.

And now I was following my high school bully to...who knew where exactly.

10

MIGUEL

As Emry Black walked half a step behind me, following me to the staff headquarters, it was time for a quick recap. I needed to do one to steady myself against the dizziness I'd been feeling since stepping out onto that stage tonight.

So...my first-ever comedy show (and I'm using the word *comedy* incredibly loosely here) tanked and was the biggest debacle of my life, and now the kid I had bullied and thought I had accidentally killed after he got struck by lightning in a field that I sent him out to was not only alive but right here with me.

Emry hadn't changed a lot since I'd seen him last, except for...becoming even more beautiful than I remembered him being. He tried to keep to himself in high school and stay under the radar. Smart move. Small-town Texas wasn't exactly accepting of gay people, much less gay people like Emry. Guys who were feminine.

I always felt bad that Jeremy, Ray, Sam, and I picked on Emry. Connor, though, he was a whole other story, next-level mean and crazy. I hadn't heard jack from any of them since we graduated. And that was just the way I wanted to keep it. We'd been douchebags of the worst kind. There was nothing more gutless than picking on someone who was an easy target. No one ever stood up for Emry, and to his credit, Emry never cowered from who he was. Not even for a second.

I did my best to try and not make it any worse, but my silence was complicity. I knew that then, and I felt it even more now that I'd had a few years to mature and grow up a bit. I could hear Emry's footsteps behind me as I led him from the bar, down a pathway past the main pool area and toward the staff bungalow. He'd been hanging out with Leo and the others, so I was sure he'd be fine to join us.

His warm breath tickled the back of my neck, reminding me of his presence. As if I could forget. I honestly thought he had died that night. His family was so mysterious about it. He didn't attend graduation (which was to be expected), and it became this huge mystery about town. What in the world had happened to Emry

Black? I left shortly after, too, in part to escape my insufferable guilt as well as a misguided attempt at reconnecting with my heritage.

For all the torment I made him suffer, I had done my best to submit myself to something even worse. I knew I couldn't compare the two, and there was no justification or excuse for what I had done to him, but in the absence of anyone else to punish me, I took it upon myself to make sure I never forgot.

"Where are we going?" Emry's voice floated in the air between us, mixing with the sweet scents of the tropical flowers that surrounded us.

I stopped and he almost crashed into me. As I spun around to face him, I was struck by how close we were. So close I could see the glints of moonlight that beamed in his eyes. My chest cinched and my senses scattered as he peered up at me from behind his long lashes.

I could hear the words in my mind. They were very simple words, and there were only a handful of them. *Up to staff headquarters.* That was all I had to say, but could I? No.

I was dumbstruck, overcome with a sudden torrent of emotions: relief, guilt, sadness, shame, confusion, and...something else. A feeling that teetered just outside my emotional periphery, dancing in shadows so dark that not even the glow of the moon could reach them. I knew enough that it was there, but I couldn't sharpen it to see it, bring it into focus.

"Miguel?"

It was the first time he'd called me by my new name.

"Are you feeling okay?"

I managed to nod. "Yeah, uh, just follow me." I turned to start walking, then changed my mind and twisted again, only to bump into Emry, who had begun to follow me. Our chests collided, and my heart let out a flurry of hiccupped beats.

"Staff headquarters." I strangled the words out of my throat to answer his earlier question about where we were going. Then I added, "You're safe."

Emry looked taken aback. I winced. Shit. Maybe I shouldn't have drawn attention to the fact that he hadn't been safe with me for so many years. I just wanted to assure him that this wasn't like that.

I wasn't excusing what had happened, and I sure as hell didn't want to sweep it under the rug, I just needed to let him know that we were two different people in a very different situation now.

"I know." His tone was soft, yet carried an unmissable defiance. That part of him hadn't changed, either.

We walked past the pool and down the narrow pebble stone trail in silence. I snuck in discreet, furtive glances whenever I could, hoping he wouldn't see it, needing to confirm that he was real. That this was really happening. It was. And I had no idea how to feel about any of it.

We arrived at the bungalow that Leo had set aside as staff headquarters and were met with a scene that looked like a party. Music was playing, staff were mingling and talking merrily. Joel approached Emry and I as soon as we stepped in and handed us both a red cup with who knew what in it. I didn't wait to ask, throwing it back as soon as it landed in my hand.

"Fuuuuck," I hissed. "What is in that?"

"Vodka with a splash of soda," he replied with a wry smile. "Figured you'd need it."

Our eyes met. "I'll be needing more than just one. Keep 'em coming, please."

Emry and I broke off shortly after that. His friend—I didn't know his name, but I'd seen him hanging out with Leo, so I guessed they were friends—came over and practically scooped Emry into his muscular arms and took him away from me. He shot me a filthy look, no doubt his silent feedback about my act. Can't say I blamed him, really.

Joel returned with another drink and I took another big swig. "How bad was it?" I asked, wiping my mouth with the back of my hand to clean up the overshot I had hastily taken.

He leaned against the wall. "It was impressive."

"How so?"

Joel cracked a smile. "Well, you managed to find a way to offend white folks, women, gay men, straight men...basically anyone with half a brain cell, really."

I grumbled into my now empty red cup. I'd just downed my second drink and was still feeling as shitty as when I was stone-cold sober. When would the magic of alcohol kick in? My eyes scanned the scene, until I stopped, hit in the face by the realization of what I was doing: searching for Emry.

The bungalow was like the before shot you saw on those TV renovation shows. It was built in the '80s, and well, let's just say there's a reason why people still refer to that decade as the one that good style forgot. Gaudy neons sat alongside nauseating pastels whichever way you looked. A chunky TV gathered dust in the corner, garish tiles lined the floor, and the walls were adorned with tropical palm wallpaper. Yes, three words that should officially be banished forever from the English language.

Leo had undertaken a massive renovation of the resort last year, modernizing the place so that the rooms and features matched the impressive location on the crest of the Gulf of Mexico and the world-famous Floridian hospitality we offered here. But this bungalow remained untouched. He insisted on it, and I knew why. It was his and Dante's special place.

Emry was in the kitchen, standing with his friend, Leo, and a small group of staff members from other departments. I reluctantly made my way over to them. Daniel, from reception, was carrying around a tray of green-colored shots just as I reached the group. Leo handed them out to all of us. Then an awkward silence hit.

"To making mistakes," he announced, raising his shot. "And to letting them go."

Emry's eyes found me, pinning me with such force that I felt I would topple over any moment. Okay, so maybe the magic of alcohol was starting to take effect. We threw our shots back, but immediately, our gazes returned to each other.

Leo turned to face me and began consoling me, as the group around us splintered into their own side conversations. I was starting to feel a little hazy, having to lean against the countertop to steady myself. I'd been busy focusing on Leo, trying to take in the encouragement he was giving me, when I felt a warmth radiating from my left side.

I flicked my head over and it was Emry. He was still talking to his friend—the one who looked like he wanted to punch me in the face—but I felt a wave of relief wash over me that he'd ended up beside me. Our elbows knocked gently against each other.

We both turned and said, "Sorry," to each other at the same time.

A shiver of exhilaration raced up my spine. *Whoa, what the hell was that?* Okay, the buzz was definitely kicking in, and if I didn't slow down, it would kick my butt.

So, naturally, I yelled out, "More shots!"

"Maybe you should slow down a little there," Leo advised as Daniel returned, and I lifted two more shots off the tray. Leo shook his head as I handed him one.

"I'll take it," a voice from my left said.

I turned and Emry was looking at me, a smile playing on the edges of his lips, as he looked at the shots I was holding in my hands.

"Oh, of course." I handed him the small plastic cup, our fingers grazing against each other. It was the second time we'd physically touched in as many minutes, and damn, if it didn't leave me with a knotty hunger for more.

We shot back the drinks, our gazes glued to each other, before returning to our respective conversations.

Leo leaned in a little closer. "Miguel, what are you doing?"

"What does it look like?" I replied with a defeated shrug. "I want to get so blind drunk so that I don't feel any worse about what just happened."

"You won't feel any better by drinking yourself to oblivion. Believe me," he cautioned.

I knew he was right, but I didn't care. I wasn't up for long-term thinking, and yes, tomorrow morning counted as long-term.

The ghosts of my past had just caught up to my failed dreams, so what was a guy to do except call out for even more shots? Followed by more and more...and yep, even more.

By the time there were no more shots left to drink, I was beyond buzzing. The countertop had fallen over, so it was completely useless to me. In fact, the whole room was slanted on a weird angle. Hmm, we really needed to get maintenance onto that.

As I took a step—forward, I think—I felt the heat of another hand on me. I looked to my left and saw Emry's pretty face, and his pretty eyes, and his pretty lips. He was so pretty and all of his prettiness was pointed at me. Oh, I saw what was happening here— he was helping me walk.

Oh, shit. I was drunk. Like, ridiculously skunk drunk.

And as the two of us moved—to where, I had no idea—all I could think about was how nice it was that pretty Emry Black had stayed by my side the whole night. I blinked heavily a few times, and right before everything faded to black, I felt my cheeks burning from the wide grin that had plastered itself onto my face.

SATURDAY

11
EMRY

The sofa springs that had found a home in my lower back muscles creaked as I attempted to roll over. Not that there was much of anything to roll over onto. I didn't know if he'd done it deliberately when furniture shopping, but Miguel was the owner of the world's smallest and most uncomfortable couch.

A groggy yawn escaped me as I scrubbed a palm over my face. My back ached, I hadn't slept well, and the room was way too brightly lit for what I assumed was still way too early. It would take a lot of coffee beans to put the *good* into this *morning*.

At least I'd made sure Miguel had gotten home safely last night. Even though Leo, and a number of the other guys had offered to do it, part of me wanted to be the one to take him home. I insisted. And believe me, I could be fiercely determined when I set my mind to it.

But *why* did I want to do it so much? I didn't have an answer to that question...yet. All I knew was that as I saw Miguel deteriorating into a drunken mess beside me last night, I wanted to reach out and help.

But I didn't.

I held back. Not out of shyness, but because it felt like he needed that moment to process the aftermath of his show. My presence had only unsteadied his already rocky footing even more. So I stayed near him all night, and when he'd finally had enough, that's when I stepped in to help.

My back made a creaking sound I wasn't expecting to hear for at least another twenty years as I propped myself into a seated position on the couch, curling my feet underneath me. I looked around the small apartment, my eyes flickering over the dust particles that shone as the sunlight streamed in.

The place was small but tidy. The open-plan layout meant that the living, dining, and kitchen areas were visible from where I was. An opening to the right of the kitchen revealed the start of a hallway, which I assumed led to the rest of the apartment.

Just as I was about to get up and go to the bathroom, I heard a door creak open. Then, footsteps. Each one accompanied by a painful groan. Miguel shlomped into the room, his face hidden behind his palm.

Before he could open his mouth to speak, he toppled over something on the floor, his arms flew wide, and two awkward half-steps later, he backed over the couch and tumbled down next to me. If he'd incorporated some slapstick physical comedy into his routine like this, it might have gone down a bit better. Though I decided to keep that critique to myself.

Keeping a straight face, I asked, "How are you feeling?"

Two rheumy eyes looking back at me gave me my answer. "Like horse shit," Miguel managed to croak.

The poor guy looked like he was nursing the world's worst hangover. He needed a glass of water. I shot up onto my feet and that's when his bleary eyes widened. His gaze was fixed on my torso. My naked torso. I looked down the length of my body. Hey, at least I was wearing underwear.

He coughed up a lung, his face and neck reddening. "What happened last night?" he spluttered.

"I have no idea." I looked into his watery eyes. I'd had a few too many drinks, too, but I knew well enough that after I put Miguel to his bed, the only action I had gotten was from his couch springs, which seemed fixated on poking me in all sorts of places.

"Don't worry. Nothing happened. I mean, we're still wearing underwear, right?" I offered with a grin.

"Yeah." Miguel's lips were stretched in a wiry smirk. "Each other's."

Holy crap, he was right. How the heyyy did that happen? Miguel went back to rubbing his face like he could somehow scrub away the memories of last night, while I brushed my hand through my hair and tried to make sense of the whole underwear situation.

A vague memory of us having "one last drink" after we tumbled through his front door rang in the back of my mind. It was more of a challenge than anything else, really. That might have been followed by an underwear switch dare Miguel lobbed my way, too. But nothing more. And no sex. Definitely no sex. That much I was certain of.

The original plan had been for me to Uber back to the resort after making sure Miguel had made it home safely. But, yeah, that obviously didn't happen. Again, something made me stay, wanting to be near him. I didn't want to revisit the past, but I did have some questions.

Like why the hell was he called Miguel?

I sashayed into the kitchen and brought him back a glass of water. He took it from me appreciatively. "Thank you," he said after he'd taken a few sips, his voice starting to return to normal.

I stood in front of him, unsure of what to do next. My stomach growled and Miguel's lips twitched. "You hungry?"

I nodded, suddenly very aware that I was standing in front of him in his apartment wearing only underwear. *His* underwear. "Yeah."

His eyes lingered on me and it was like they were lasers because I felt my skin prickling with heat under the soft gaze. "There's a good breakfast joint just around the corner. They do killer pancakes."

My stomach rumbled again. This time, Miguel laughed and a warmth infiltrated his dark eyes. I realized it was the first time I'd heard his laughter. Ever.

A cold shiver ran down my spine. What was I doing here? Was this a mistake? Yes, we were both adults now, but back then, he was part of a pack that had been hell-bent on making my life miserable.

I should have said no to his offer of breakfast, but given the lack of caffeine in my system, not to mention the lingering haziness of last night's alcohol over-consumption, I found myself nodding instead.

"Good." Miguel drained the water and sat up a little taller. "I have the hangover from hell, and I'm assuming you have some questions?"

I nodded again.

He stood up and I resisted the urge to step back. He was only a couple of inches taller than me, but it was still enough to feel slightly imposing. Not that there was anything threatening or menacing about his demeanor. If anything, his behavior was pointing to a genuine friendliness. But, you know, muscle memory and all that.

"Why don't you jump in the shower first? There are clean towels in the bathroom."

I tipped my head and brushed past him. He caught me, hooking his fingers into the crook of my elbow. "Thank you, Emry."

The glinting depths of his dark irises revealed nothing, leaving me to wonder what was going on behind them.

Twenty minutes later, we were seated in a window booth at the diner just down the block from his apartment. We hadn't talked a whole lot. For my part, I was silent because I was trying to figure out what was going on for me. The pull I had felt so strongly to be near him last night was teetering under the broad daylight of a new day.

My feelings were jumbled up. Miguel was part of my past. A bad part of a very troubled past. It was stirring up sediment on my emotional floor that I preferred to keep matted down. But I couldn't deny that I was intrigued by him. Curious to know where life had taken him since leaving Blessing and what was with that damn name change.

But as our double order of pancakes arrived and I was just about to ask him that very question, he beat me to it. "How are you still alive, Emry?"

Oh, right. That whole *getting struck by a bolt of lightning* thing.

"What do you want to know?" It wasn't a defensive question. I just wanted to know what he knew about it. People in Blessing liked to gossip. I could only imagine some of the wild stories that had come out of that night.

"All of it," Miguel replied as he barreled a forkful of pancake into his mouth. "I don't know anything other than you got struck by lightning and then vanished."

I placed my fork at the side of my plate. This was going to be a long story. "Well, I guess it started with me running through Ol' Man Jerry's field to escape…"

"Me and my douchebag buddies." Miguel filled in the awkward silence for me. I didn't know how to finish that sentence, so I was glad he had done it for me.

"Yeah." I squirmed a little in my seat. I wasn't good at talking about this. Up until now, I hadn't needed to. But he wanted to know, and considering he thought he had killed me, I figured he deserved to know what had really happened that night.

"Anyway, it was storming and with my great luck, as I was running through the field, I heard a huge cracking sound. A big flash of light came from the sky, barreling straight at me. It hit me."

Miguel stopped eating, his fork dangling off his fingers as he took it all in. "You remember all of this?"

I wish I hadn't, but I did. "Yeah," I gave a slight nod. "I do. Every bit of it. I can still recall every millisecond of it right now, even as I'm sitting here talking to you. Even after all these years, it feels as real and as vivid as anything that happened yesterday."

I paused for a beat before continuing. "The force of the strike threw me backward like a ragdoll, and then"—my breath trembled —"and then something really weird happened."

Miguel leaned in closer. "What?" His eyes were glued to me, hanging on to every word of my almost unbelievable story.

"As I was being flung backward, I had this really strong sensation that I was actually being pushed forward. I remember looking out at the trees on the right side of the field by the fence line, and they were moving like I was going straight ahead, but I could feel myself getting thrown backward. It was the weirdest sensation I'd ever felt in my life until..."

Even reliving it now, my body was buzzing with anxious energy. My fingertips fluttered against the top of the table, and my chest felt heavy. Memories squeezed at my lungs, making it almost impossible to breathe.

I glanced over and was met by two football-sized eyeballs. "Until what, Emry?"

"Until I landed on the ground."

"Why? What happened then?"

This was the part that still freaked me out. Hence my whole, you know, avoidance thing. "Once I hit the ground, I remember looking at myself from, like, ten feet away. I thought I was dead and having an out of body experience."

Miguel took a swig of his water. "What was that like?"

"Weird." There was no other word for it, really. "Because as I was out of my body, it dawned on me that I was still thinking and feeling as if I were still in my body. I had this big realization that wherever I am, I'm still always me. Kooky, huh?"

Miguel's face was strained in an attempt to make sense of this whole crazy story. He was mulling it over in his head. "No," he answered after a few moments, but didn't elaborate.

We both returned to our food for a bit. "What happened next?" he asked around a mouthful of pancakes.

"That's when things start to get a bit hazy for me. After a few moments of looking at my body from out of my body, I felt like the part of me that was doing the observing started to dissolve, piece by piece. I just went up, not in a puff of smoke, but from my feet up. I gradually disintegrated until that me was entirely gone. Only a ball of energy remained and I had this sense that I was floating without gravity, like astronauts do in space."

Miguel and I looked at each other at the exact same moment. A tender curiosity simmered in his eyes. I cleared my throat and continued, "That weightless feeling lasted, I don't know, maybe a few seconds. I'm not sure how time fit into any of this. And then it was like someone flipped a switch, and I was fully back in my body, and I hated it."

"Why?"

"Oh my guuurrl." I unfurled my fingers in the air for dramatic effect. "The pain. It was terrible. Everything hurt, every muscle, bone, my skin felt like it was on fire. My head, where the lightning struck and my foot, where it left me, felt like I was being poked by a hot iron."

"I can't even imagine."

My story was clearly putting Miguel off his food, as he lowered his fork and stopped eating.

"Anyway, that's where my memory ends," I said with a shrug to loosen some of the tension that had bunched up in my back and across my shoulders. "Someone driving by saw what happened and called 9 1 1. I got taken to the local hospital. Then they transferred me to Houston, and the next thing I remember was waking up in my uncle's apartment in Philadelphia."

Miguel's dark brows cramped together. "What about your parents? You didn't go back to your own home?"

I looked down at my plate. I'd done more food moving than eating. "No."

"So, what happened after that?"

I was glad Miguel didn't press me on that anymore. I didn't feel like delving into how my parents basically used my accident as their opportunity to wipe their hands of me, conveniently shipping me off to my uncle and never seeing me again. Ironically, I'd been making plans to stay with him after graduation, anyway. But in a slightly more healthy state.

"Let's see." I twined the metal fork between my fingers. "It took me about a week for the fog to lift, but when it did, I couldn't remember things like people's names, places, objects. It was all...gone."

"Shit."

"Um, so yeah, that was kinda scary."

"I bet."

"But as my body healed and my burn marks faded, my memory came back. About a month later, while I was still taking it easy but moving around okay, I had this huge desire to listen to classical music."

"I never knew you liked classic music."

I shook my head. "I didn't. Unless you counted '80s Madonna."

"That's not classical." Miguel perked up. "That's ancient."

We both giggled, which helped suck up some of the awkwardness I'd been feeling as I'd been reliving this story with him.

"My uncle had some classical records, like the old-school vinyl ones, and I started listening to them nonstop. I streamed every classical station and playlist on Spotify. I couldn't get enough of it. Then one day, I had this sudden urge to go up to the grand piano he had in his study. I sat down and I just played. Everything that I'd been listening to just poured out of me, shooting straight through my fingers and onto the keys. Not a single note out of whack. I did it for, like, a minute, maybe two."

"Had you played piano before?"

"Nope, never," I said emphatically.

"That's...insane."

I rocked my head in agreement. "Tell me about it. Anyways, to make a long story slightly shorter, over time, I became able to play for longer and longer stretches. One night, my uncle was throwing a soiree—"

"A soiree?" Miguel's eyebrows lifted as his eyes shimmered with a playfulness I hadn't ever seen on him before.

"Yes, a soiree. My uncle was fancy like that." I let out another light giggle. "Anyway, I started playing and one of the guys there happened to be the conductor for The Philadelphia Orchestra. And, so yeah, that's kinda what happened to me after I left Blessing and how I became a pianist."

"Wait. You play the piano now? For a living?"

"Yep."

"Whoa..." Miguel fell against the back of the booth. "That's an incredible story, Emry."

It was. I placed my fingers on the table and stretched them out wide. I'd been doing a helluva lot of talking.

Now it was time for me to fire back with a question of my own.

12

MIGUEL

I couldn't believe I was sharing a booth with Emry Black. The last night I'd seen him alive, he had been coming out of a diner, too. And now here we were, years later. Him, alive and me *feeling* like death. What the hell was I thinking last night, drinking myself into oblivion like that? Oh, that's right. I wasn't.

Emry's story filled the gaps in my head that weren't pounding with a thunderous ache. Bottom line: I hadn't killed him or even injured him too seriously. Yes, he still went through it, but by the sounds of things, he'd come out the other side better than ever.

Thank.

God.

That night had never drifted too far away from me. I'd been able to recollect it all too easily, and I did...all too frequently.

I remembered urging Emry to run off into the field. I did it for his own protection, and if I had to do it all again, I would. Seeing Connor's pickup pulling up the main street in a menacing crawl and knowing what kind of foul mood he'd been in that day, I was worried for Emry's safety.

Turned out, my fears were justified.

Connor flashed his beams at me when he spotted me on the sidewalk. Thankfully, that was after Emry had taken my advice and run off. I felt a heavy pit form in my gut as I approached Connor's truck. "Get in." I could still remember his pissed-off snarl as if it were yesterday.

His voice was rough, and his face sported a bright red shiner. A new one. Probably courtesy of his father. It'd been a good three days since he'd shown up to school, which usually meant that his dad was hitting the bottle...and then him.

We drove around aimlessly in the storm, neither one of us wanting to go home. Funny, for a bully that made fun of Emry for being gay and effeminate, Connor was the first guy I ever went down on.

It was kind of our sick, twisted routine—pick on gay kids or anyone who was slightly different at school during the day, get

together and hook up in secret at night. I lived in the second to last
house at the end of a dead-end street. A block away, there was an
empty, overgrown lot. That was our spot. Connor would pull in
behind the thick wall of trees, cut the engine and lights, and I'd give
him head. Always me blowing him, never the other way around.

But that stormy night, as lightning flashed around us and the
hefty drops of rain drowned out his low grunts, something was off
with him. He was rougher with me than he'd ever been, pulling my
hair and making me gag on him.

The sick, twisted thing was that I was aching hard the whole
time. I knew he was only using me, and I was getting off on it. After
he dropped me home, I ran into my bedroom, pressed my back
against the door (my parents didn't believe in door locks), and
jerked myself off to a cummy oblivion.

The shame that flooded me as soon as I finished was
overbearing and prickly. There must've been something seriously
wrong with me to have gotten off on being used like that. There
was no other explanation for it. I'd carefully locked those feelings
away into a *never to be opened* drawer.

And now, seated across the table from Emry, those and a
million other feelings were returning, threatening to overwhelm me
in my already fragile hungover state.

I snuck a glance at Emry. He had just finished telling me his
amazing story and was reaching for a sip of water. Sunlight danced
across his cute features, and I picked up on a strange subtlety I'd
never seen in him.

He was a femme guy. Camp. Flamboyant. And because of that,
everything he said and did and wore was so extra. Big. Loud. Bold.
But right now, in this moment, his bigness mixed with a subdued,
steely resolve, and a strength that didn't need to be acknowledged
with words was coming through.

I'd been wrong to pick on Emry in high school, and I'd be
stupid to underestimate Emry now. Despite his clothes,

mannerisms, and makeup, one thing was becoming crystal clear to me: Emry Black was more of a man than I could ever hope to be.

I couldn't take back what I had done to him, the role I had played in trying to make him feel like shit just because I felt like shit and didn't know how to deal with it. I took stuff out on him to deflect from me—from being a slightly pudgy kid of immigrant parents who tried their best to keep up with the image of a happy American family, but fell short.

Just as a years-long and way overdue apology bubbled up my throat to the edge of my tongue, Emry spoke. "So, why did you change your name? You were Michael Cordon in high school."

His eyelids flickered momentarily, and as I looked at his hand cupping the water tumbler, I noticed a slight tremble. "I'm remembering that correctly, right?"

I could barely manage to swallow, my throat deserted of moisture. "You are."

I was going to have to tell him. How could I not after what he'd shared with me? The thing was, I'd never said these words out loud to anyone before. I'd never needed to. My life was conveniently split into two parts, two very distinct and separate worlds. One belonged to Michael Cordon, the other to Miguel Cortez. And they never, ever mixed together.

Until right now.

"You don't have to tell me about it if you don't want to." A sympathetic smile accompanied his offer.

But I did, and we both kind of knew it. And what was even more bizarre, part of me actually wanted to let him in on this part of my life.

"My parents are from El Salvador." I started with the easy part —blaming my parents.

"Oh, I never knew that."

I gave a tight nod. "Then it worked."

A frown creased Emry's expression. "What worked?"

"Fooling everyone into thinking that we were just your average American family. My parents were obsessed with it."

"I don't understand, sorry."

I sucked a deep breath in. "Neither do I, but I guess they just wanted to put their past behind them and focus on a future. Here, in America. And you know, being brown isn't always super easy in this country, and..."

God, I couldn't believe I was actually going to be saying this. "Well, we weren't *that* brown, you know? We could get away with not getting clocked for it. Mom dyed her hair blonde, and Dad was fair-skinned. If I stayed out of the sun, I was actually pretty pale, too. Sure, dark hair and eyes, but, you know, passable."

"Passable?" There was a sadness in the way Emry echoed the word that hit me right between the eyes.

"So, anyway, I always hated the fact that they were like that. I mean, in a way, I got it. Life was hard for them in El Salvador. I don't know all the details, but my dad was a journalist, and I get the impression he got on the government's bad side. From what I've been able to piece together, I think they kinda had to leave for their own safety."

"Oh, shit."

"Yeah. So I get that part. But, now that we were here, in America, it's like they wanted to erase all memories of our heritage, while I wanted to at least know something about it. Nothing could change that was where we were from. I love living in this country, but that doesn't mean I didn't have a right to know about where I was born."

"Hablas español?" His voice sounded even cuter in Spanish.

I shook my head vehemently. "*Nooo*. Our household was English-only. Why? Do you?"

Emry shrugged in a way that indicated he did, but didn't want to make a big deal about it. "A little. Enough to get by."

"I did go back, though. To El Salvador."

"You did. When?" Emry picked up a fork and went back to finishing his by now cold pancakes.

"Straight after graduation. I had saved up some money during high school and bought a plane ticket with it. All of our extended family had remained there: grandparents, aunts, uncles, cousins... I thought it would be like this wonderful family reunion. I'd be embraced with open arms and could settle there, at least for a little while. Learn the language, learn about my history, see how I fitted into the bigger picture of my family tree."

Emry slowed his chewing down. "So, what happened?"

I squirmed in my seat. I didn't want to get into this part. The hurt of it had never left me entirely. How despite being blood, my family felt like total strangers to me. How even though I wanted to return to my roots, seeing the poverty and violence up close and personal was actually really scary and made me long to come back to my actual home: America.

"Can I tell you some other time?"

"Oh, of course." Emry bolted upright in his seat. "I'm sorry, Miguel. I didn't mean to make you uncomfortable."

I scratched the back of my neck. "Thanks. Anyway, to answer your question about my name. I changed it before I left. It was my first step to reclaiming my identity. Miguel Cortez was my birth name."

Emry's overcompensating wide smile warmed me a little. "Miguel Cortez. That's a really nice name. It suits you."

"Thanks. And, you know, it has the added bonus of fitting in with my current career."

"I don't get it," Emry said.

"You know, a housekeeper called Miguel. It kinda fits the stereotype."

Emry propped his elbow onto the table and his chin slid into his palm. He smoothed his fingertips along his cheek as he shot me a deep, contemplative look, his eyes turning mossy green. "Don't let yourself be defined by stereotypes, Miguel. There's always more to a person than what's on the surface."

I nodded, stupidly, as I cringed at my lame-ass attempt at humor. It was obvious he wasn't just talking about me, though. In that moment, I wanted to ask him so many more questions. But it wasn't the right time. There were things both of us weren't ready to say to each other yet.

I gobbled up the remaining soggy pancakes on my plate. "So, it sounds like you're super successful and I clean up people's dirty sheets for a living."

Emry blushed. I didn't know how he'd respond to that. I didn't know what response I was expecting or even hoping for. My headache was dimming, but I wasn't anywhere near back to full operating capacity.

He ignored my self-deprecating comment and volleyed back a question that caught me completely by surprise after it had tumbled out of his mouth.

"Want to have dinner with me tonight, Miguel?"

13

EMRY

"*Oooh,* I'll have a Drill it Into My Hole, please." I shot the bartender a cheeky smile, before nudging Hawk, who was studying Elysian's new drink menu carefully.

"Half the fun is reading the cocktail names," he muttered without even looking up.

Brad, the bartender, leaned in and pointed to the drink listed at the top of the laminated page. "That one was my idea."

"Your Dad's Dick Was Better," Hawk read it out loud, letting out a low chuckle. "Slightly controversial, but I like it."

I leaned over to get a better view and started reading a few of them aloud, too.

"Don't Ignore My Balls, Bossy Bottom—"

"That one goes well with a Chubby Chaser," Brad interjected.

"Good to know." I continued scanning the menu. "Fuck Me Like You Know My Name, I'm Straight Bro...Wait, what does this one mean, Futanari?"

Brad smiled knowingly. "It's Japanese animated porn that features transsexual or intersex characters."

I shot Hawk an impressed glance. "See...not just a drink menu, but educational, too."

We laughed, and after all that rigmarole, Hawk ordered a beer. We looked around the pool as Brad prepared our drinks. Elysian had an amazing swimup bar smack bang in the center of the pool. It meant that you could get your refreshment on without having to get up and out of the water. Genius, really.

"So I noticed you didn't get in last night."

I was too busy trying to sit myself upright in the submerged stools we were seated at to pay too much attention to the harsh bite in Hawk's tone.

"Yeah, I crashed at Miguel's. It was late and I was tired."

A muscle ticked in the side of his jaw. "Uh-huh. Where'd you sleep, in his bed?"

"On his couch, thank you very much." I kept my tone light, but then I remembered Miguel's comedy act. Oh, so *that's* why Hawk was being so...hawky about things.

"He feels terrible about the show," I explained in an attempt to allay his concerns as Brad handed us our drinks.

Hawk mumbled something into his beer but I missed it. If I didn't know any better, I'd say he was borderline sulking with the way his shoulders slumped over his drink. But we were kinda half-floating at the swimup bar, so he was just probably hulking over the bar in an attempt not to drift away.

"I do have something I need to tell you."

Hawk flicked his eyes on me. "Yeah?" He uttered the word cautiously.

"Yeah. It turns out I actually know Miguel."

I could feel his squinted eyes boring into me. He swiveled his body around so that he faced me straight on, his sizable chest heaving deeply with every steady breath he took. "How?"

"He's from Blessing, too. We, uh, went to the same high school."

Hawk didn't tend to pry too much into my personal life. So maybe I'd get away with leaving it there.

"Were you friends with him?"

Damn. No such luck this time.

"Not exactly."

I brought the Drill it Into My Hole to my lips. Hawk's eyes remained focused on me over the rim of the glass. "Actually, he was one of the bullies that teased me for being gay and..." I swiped my hand in front of me, "...like this."

"Asshole," Hawk snarled, and if he'd been gripping his glass any tighter, it would have shattered into tiny smithereens.

I let the gentle sweet burn of my drink swill around in the back of my throat. "It's...complicated."

"How so?"

I could tell this latest piece of information only elevated Hawk's protectiveness over me. He'd already had a bad feeling about the guy based on his performance last night. Now, I'd added this huge revelation to the mix. Maybe that wasn't such a smart move on my part.

I rested my drink on the edge of the bar. "I don't know how to feel about it." My heavy words contrasted sharply with the brightness of the sunny day and the sounds of happy guests swimming and frolicking around us. Oh, that's right. We were on vacation. I'd almost forgotten about that.

"Do you want to talk about it?"

I turned to face Hawk. He really was a good guy. I knew we'd started off as failed fuck buddies, and then we'd progressed to dick twins, but despite the sexual nature that permeated through most of our history, it was his friendship that meant the most to me. Especially now, when I really didn't know what was going on inside me. Still, I didn't come here to unpack my past, I'd come here to relax, get my tan on, and parade my latest fashion masterpieces around the resort.

"You know how I feel about my past," I reminded him as I placed my hand over his broad shoulder. "I don't like talking about it. It belongs right where I keep it—permanently in my rearview mirror."

"Fair enough. I get that." Hawk drained the remainder of his beer. "Wanna join me on an expedition?"

That was code for *did I want to go dick twinning?*

"If you don't—especially after what happened with that dickhead yesterday—we don't have to. I'm happy grabbing some lounges and just hanging out here with you for the day."

"I might pass," I said, mulling it over. Not because of yesterday's unsuccessful attempt, but because I felt too wobbly on the inside. I needed some time to think. "But you go ahead."

"I—I." Hawk scratched his cheek, but whatever words were on the tip of his tongue stayed there as he snapped his mouth shut. He rocked his body, as if gearing himself up for...something.

"All right," he announced, pushing off the bar and floating into the crystal blue water. "I'm off hunting." He was swimming away from me, so I couldn't see his face, but his words fell flat.

"Have fun," I yelled out after him as he splashed away.

I turned back around and caught Brad's attention. "Another one, please."

14

MIGUEL

I swear gay men had a secret psycho-sensory ability that the world didn't know about. Because of course on one of the rare days that I dragged my sorry, hungover ass into work, everything that could have possibly gone wrong did.

A leaking toilet flooded the bathroom in one of the poolside rooms, two staff had called in sick, though I had a sneaking suspicion that they were even more hungover than I was, and newbie Chase? The poor guy'd had quite the eye-opening experience. He'd accidentally walked in on a couple mid-fuck. Worse, he freaked out when they invited him to join in. There was nowhere in the employee manual that covered what to do in *that* situation. He was still clearly ruffled by it as he stood in front of my desk.

"I just didn't know whether I should report it. Is there some sort of form I could fill out?"

I suppressed my lips from moving. "No. We don't have a *I just walked in on two guys fucking* form. But I'll speak to Leo about it."

"Three." Chase's wide eyes landed on me. "There were *three* guys fucking."

Okay, it was obvious that this had rattled him and I needed to respect that. I guess I'd worked here long enough to have become immune to the sexual sights you stumbled upon serendipitously as you went about your day. I'd seen it all—sex toys left scattered in the bathroom, guys jerking off in the gym sauna, erect dicks of all shapes, sizes, and colors paraded all around the place. I'd even once stumbled in on a guest who was a yoga instructor. Let's just say if I had the ability to pretzel my body like that and reach my own dick with my lips, I'd never leave my room, either.

I might have escaped the worst of the headache, but my overall disposition was still somewhat hazy. "How are you feeling, Chase?" I asked as he settled into the chair. "Are you okay with what you saw?"

"Oh, yeah. I have no problem with it." He looked and sounded genuine, so I believed him. "I just don't want to get in trouble, like it was my fault. I knocked several times. There was no *Do Not Disturb* sign hanging off the doorknob. I did everything right."

Ah, so that's what his issue was. He thought he'd done something wrong. "You did the right thing, Chase," I confirmed and instantly, his shoulders fell and his whole disposition relaxed. "And as we tell all employees that start working with us here, this comes as part of the deal working at an all-male resort. Our guests come here for a variety of reasons. One of them is sex. We're not here to judge or make anyone feel uncomfortable. At the same time, this is your workplace and you have a right not to be made to feel uncomfortable, either. You can always come to me and talk about anything you want, okay?"

Chase nodded, his face suddenly flushed with a little sheepishness which I was determined to erase.

"Guests will test out boundaries with you. They might flirt or tease. Heck, they might ask you straight up if you wanna fuck. And you have every right to respond in whatever way feels right for you. If you want to say no, then feel free to say it. Politely, but with enough firmness to be clear about it. And if you want to go ahead with some...sexy shenanigans...just make sure you're off the clock, okay?"

Chase grinned and got to his feet. "Got it." As he reached to open the door, he turned back to look at me. "Thanks, Miguel. You're the best."

I smiled until he left and then I slumped into my chest. I felt like the worst. I was hungover. My comedy dreams were in tatters. And I'd come face to face with the person who had been haunting my memories for years.

And it wasn't even midday.

I responded to a few emails and looked over next month's roster. Marnus and Pierce had each requested a week off—at the same time—which was a little intriguing since we teased Marnus about being the token straight staff member of the group, while Pierce claimed to hate Marnus more than "Taylor hated Kanye."

Unfortunately for me, I'd forgotten to factor in their leave applications, which meant I had some shuffling to do. I decided it could wait until my brain had enough power to be able to deftly handle a spreadsheet. It wasn't there yet.

Instead, I got up and headed to Jack and Ari's suite. I'd texted them earlier to see what time worked for them for their daily cleaning service and they said anytime after eleven. I made my way through the resort, smiling politely at any guests I encountered.

I skimmed the edge of the pool area. I could get to the other side without going straight through it, instead veering down a narrow, tree-lined pathway that snaked behind the last row of deckchairs. It took a little longer, but I preferred to stay hidden, out of view. Guests didn't want to be reminded of something as dull as housekeeping when they were on vacation. I totally got it.

Besides, the salty air and sunshine was doing me a world of good. Snippets of laughter and the sounds of friends catching up and hanging out wafted in the air. The DJ was already cranking some awesome tunes, the sunny dance beats uplifting the atmosphere.

As I took in the scene, my eyes were drawn into the middle of the pool. Sitting there, alone in the swimup bar, was Emry.

My heart slammed against my ribcage as I ducked behind a palm tree, hiding like a fugitive. Why I did that, I had no idea. It's not like I was doing anything wrong or like the guy could even tell I'd spotted him. He'd have to turn and squint hard in my direction to even see me. But on some level, it didn't feel right to be looking at him.

For all the talking we'd done over breakfast and the panic that had set in when I looked at the time and we sped over to the resort, I hadn't managed to get out the two words that, while pitiful and nowhere near enough, I needed to tell him: *I'm sorry.*

I curled my head out slowly from behind the trunk to study Emry. It was hard to make any discernible observations from this far away. I flipped back around and rested my head against the solid palm trunk, my chest heaving like I'd just run a marathon.

Seeing him again had come as such an unexpected shock. He was just like I'd remembered him in so many ways. But different, too, and the reaction his presence was eliciting in me was another thing I hadn't expected.

He was cute, there was no denying that. His hazel eyes were soft yet strong, framed by two perfectly manicured and bushy eyebrows. He had a slender build which I loved. Too many guys were obsessed with guys who looked like walking walls of muscle. Give me a thin twink any day of the week. And his hair, man, I didn't know how he did it, but Emry's dark blond locks were always coiffed and styled up without as much as a strand out of place. He was drop dead gorgeous.

I shook my head. Why the hell was I paying this much attention to the way the guy looked? It's not as if there was even the remotest chance of anything happening between us. And I couldn't blame him. A guy like Emry—successful, beautiful, confident in who he was—what the hell would he see in a failed-to-launch experiment like me? He could have any guy he wanted. There was no way he'd even look twice at me.

By the time I reached Jack and Ari's suite, my mood had soured even more.

"You look like shit," Jack observed wryly as the door swung open and I trudged in. I guess my fake smiling wasn't fooling him. "Big night after the show?"

I unlocked the small cupboard by the door that housed the cleaning supplies and nodded. "Something like that."

"Miguel, what's wrong?" Ari stepped into the room. His face was ghost white and for some reason, it made him apologize the second I looked at him. "Sorry, bad morning. It's the meds. Some days, they make swallowing feel hard."

"There's a joke in there," Jack chimed in. "But I am going to leave it. I can't tell which one of you looks worse to be honest."

"We saw your show last night," Ari mentioned as Jack helped him over to the sofa.

Of course they did. That was the last thing I wanted to be reminded of right now.

"It was actually funny. Biting. And perhaps a tad too...aggressive, but that would appeal to some people."

"Yeah," I whipped back as I lugged the vacuum cleaner with me. "I just wish some of those people had shown up yesterday."

"Getting booed off stage is a rite of passage for a comedian," Jack said softly as he sat down next to Ari. Both men kept their eyes on me while all I wanted was to slink out of the room and begin cleaning floors and scrubbing tiles.

"Sit down for a minute."

It'd be rude of me to reject Jack's invitation, so I placed the vacuum cleaner alongside the kitchen island and sat across from them in the living room.

"We've been together for thirty-seven years," Jack started, and something about the abrupt change in conversation shocked me out of my own head. "We've seen each other through just about everything. Ups, downs, and everything in between."

They interlocked fingers and exchanged a loving look. It made me so happy to see true love like this. Even if I knew it was out of my grasp, and even if I wasn't entirely sure where Jack was headed with this, it was a beautiful sight to see.

"The reason I'm telling you this, Miguel, is because when either one of us has made a mistake in life, the other one has been there to catch us."

"But I am painfully single," I reminded them.

"Exactly." Jack snapped his fingers, pinning me with a determined look. "Which makes it all the more important—in the absence of having a soulmate to lean on—to lean on yourself. And the load you're carrying this morning gets a hell of a lot lighter with forgiveness."

I chewed my bottom lip. His words resonated, and part of me

understood what he meant. Another part of me was blocked to that word, though. *Forgiveness.* How could I forgive myself after what I'd done last night? I'd humiliated myself something shocking.

"Thanks, Jack. I appreciate the advice," I said, rising to my feet.

He got up as well and smiled. "I've been on this planet a lot longer than you have, Miguel. Please consider what I've said. I know it's not easy, but if you can't forgive yourself, life is going to get you down. Big time."

I nodded, making my way to the cleaning equipment. Oh, believe me, I knew a thing or two about that.

15

EMRY

Despite having a whole day to think about it, I still hadn't figured out an answer to the question that was burning up my brain—why did I invite Miguel to dinner?

Turns out that Google *didn't* have an answer for everything. When I searched for *"how to react to a former high school bully who sent you out into a field where you got struck by lightning and then you run into him years later after he bombed at his first comedy show,"* I got no results. Funny that.

Even more realistic, concise searches hadn't been that helpful. I wasn't able to find a single article, blog—hell, not even a meme—that captured the whirlwind I was swept up in at running into Miguel.

I glanced up over the leather-bound menu. "Have you decided on what you would like to order?"

Elysian's restaurant was to die for. It had a Michelin star and the best, local seafood I'd ever tasted anywhere. I could see Miguel's brow pinched in concentration as his eyes darted across the menu.

"No. Not yet. I'm a little lost."

"Lost?"

"Yeah." He placed the menu carefully down on the white linen tablecloth, his dark eyes darting from left to right. "I don't usually eat at fancy places like this."

Ah, I got it. I thought he looked a little unsettled. I put it down to the shock of seeing me, and I'm sure that was part of it, too. But in addition to being great food, it was as pricey as you'd expect it to be. "This is on me. I asked you out—I mean, to join me for dinner."

The tips of his ears seared with a bright red hue and he forced a smile. "Thanks."

But even as the entrées arrived—I went for the grilled, wild-caught shrimp with gochugaru chili, garlic, and chives, while Miguel chose the steak tartare—a pent-up guardedness remained between us. Finally, Miguel put down his cutlery, stared at me with the two deepest eyes I'd ever seen and said, "I'm sorry, Emry."

I almost choked on my shrimp. I brought the napkin to my lips and before I could chime in with a response of my own, Miguel continued. "And I'm sorry that I didn't say sorry sooner. Like, this morning. Over breakfast. I wanted to, I really did, but I was still in shock, I guess, processing the fact that you were alive and well and sitting in front of me."

He took a sip of water, but lifted his index finger, a sign he was midstream and not done yet. He looked somewhere off to the side before he pointed his dark irises straight at me. "Actually, I should have manned the fuck up and called you years ago to own up to my shit and the way I treated you. Or at least tried to contact you. Heck, even Facebook-stalked you. Because you deserve an apology from me, Emry. In fact, I should be down on my knees, begging for your forgiveness over the way I treated you in high school."

I realized I'd been covering the lower half of my face with the napkin, suspended in a state of disbelief, at the words flying out of his mouth.

He stopped talking, drained his glass of water, and smoothed the front of his black shirt down with what I noticed for the first time were incredibly long, lithe fingers.

I heard his words. I did. And I heeded the painful emotions that stirred behind them. I believed that he genuinely meant every word he was saying. I appreciated the sentiment and the strength it took to apologize. I really did.

But the walls I had built up around that time in my life were so high, so impenetrable, that there was nothing he could say that would get through and breach my defenses. It wasn't about him. I'd been the one to close myself off to that part of my life the day my parents had shipped me off to my uncle's.

I was done with my family. I was done with Blessing, Texas. And I sure as heck was done with every last person from there.

Or so I thought.

But maybe I wasn't?

No. No. *No*.

I couldn't let this one chance encounter break down all those walls. Even though I made it look easy (*and fabulous, too!*), it took work, determination and effort to keep the past in the past. One slight crack, one little slip up and would all of that work be gone? I never wanted to be that kid again. I couldn't let myself slip back into that time, that victim mode, that life, ever again. I wouldn't allow it.

"Emry?"

The unsure way Miguel stuttered my name was a gentle reminder that I'd retreated into my head for maybe a little longer than I'd realized.

"Thank you for apologizing, Miguel." I sat up taller and interlaced my fingers, drumming them in a loose melody against the table.

"I know one lame-ass apology won't cut it," Miguel explained as he brushed a wayward dark strand behind his ear. "And if you never want to see me again, I totally get it. You've moved on. You have your life now, and by the sounds of it, you're totally winning at it."

His smile contained a sorrow that not even his full lips could hide. "I'm probably the last person you ever wanted to see on vacation. I get that. I really do."

"I don't hate this." I kept my eyes fixed on my fingers.

I'd spoken so softly that it forced Miguel to say, "Excuse me. I didn't quite catch that."

Slowly, as I exhaled, I looked up and into the eyes of my former high school bully and repeated, "I don't hate the fact that we ran into each other, Miguel." It still felt a little strange calling him that, but I was getting used to it the more I said it.

I tried to speak but couldn't. The words had embedded themselves on the jagged lump at the hollow of my throat. I wanted to tell him that I just didn't do *this*. I didn't stroll down memory lane. Ever. That part of my life was over, sealed up and filed away never to be reopened.

I also wanted to admit that even though, yes, he'd been part of a gang that had bullied me and made my life hell, he was always the nicest one. I knew it didn't excuse his behavior for a minute, but it mattered to me because after what he'd told me about his family life, it sounded like he'd been going through his own kind of hell, too.

I carefully studied his face and was transported to the time our eyes met in the hallway the morning of my accident. There had been something more to him then, and there was something more to him now.

Feeling his expectant gaze penetrating me, I did what I did when plan A: avoidance, wasn't an option. I defaulted to plan B: deflection.

"So"—I swallowed around the lump still stubbornly lodged in my throat—"tell me more about your comedy."

16

MIGUEL

So far, the dinner had been going swimmingly.

Okay, that was a complete and utter lie. Nothing about this evening was going well, and as usual, it was all completely my fault.

I felt so out of place at the restaurant. It didn't help that I knew all the staff so well, and for them to be serving us—*me*—it just felt all sorts of wrong. But Emry had organized it, and he was a guest on vacation, so I didn't want to burst his bubble.

Apologizing to him had felt good. Better than good, actually. It felt amazing. It wasn't like a tremendous weight had been lifted off my shoulders and I could just brush my hands and forget about what I'd done. Not at all. That would've been too unrealistic. But having the opportunity to say the words I needed to say to him— face to face, man to man—did unburden some small part of me. Just a little.

Like I'd told him, one apology—no matter how real and genuine —was only that: a single sorry. He deserved a lifetime of them from me. Which, when I thought about it, didn't sound so bad as far as self-inflicted punishments went.

But now the conversation had taken a decidedly prickly turn. We were on the topic of my failed dreams, otherwise known as my joke of a comedy career. I was pretty sure he hadn't meant it in a bad way, and he wasn't giving me any grief or judgment about the abysmal performance he'd witnessed. It almost seemed like he was genuinely curious. There was an empathy behind his gaze that caught me completely unaware.

"Not much to tell." I twisted the napkin around my index finger on my lap. "I've never done anything about it, never pursued it professionally—"

"Can I ask why?" he interrupted, his hazel eyes alive with interest.

"Um, well"—I kept fidgeting with the fray of the napkin seam under the table—"I guess the honest answer is...I was afraid. What if I didn't have any talent? What if I got up on stage for the first time and bombed so badly that my act had to get cut as I got booed off stage? Oh, wait. That *did* happen."

Emry's eyes shimmered as he stared intently at me. When I smiled at my own lighthearted remark, it was as if it gave him permission to fall into a tight smile of his own, too.

"So, I'm now firmly entrenched in the failure to launch phase of adulthood." I lifted the crumpled up napkin and threw it down onto the table beside my plate, exasperated. "That horror spectacle of a comedy show wasn't just humiliating, Emry. It was the beginning and end of my dream."

I exhaled sharply as a wet heat formed and scalded the backs of my eyes. I bit the inside of my cheek. *No.* I was not going to lose my shit here. Not in public. Not in front of Emry. That would have been the cherry on my humiliation sundae, and I was so not doing that.

A set of silky fingers smoothed over the top of my hand. I blinked in quick succession, looking at the sight of Emry's hand on mine like I'd never seen two hands touching before.

Emry spoke with a hushed reverence. "Born to blossom, bloom to perish."

"That's so me," I said as the beauty and the tragedy of the words washed over me. "Who is that? Shakespeare or Mark Twain or something?"

"Actually"—a smile drifted across his lips—"Gwen Stefani."

My mouth gaped open as Emry let out the cutest giggle I'd ever heard. He straightened up a little as he said, "Hey, we all start somewhere." His voice was warm and friendly and...pitying. Oh. Right. That's what he was doing here. Feeling sorry for me being the pathetic loser that I was. For a moment there I thought—

It didn't matter what I thought. Yet my pulse that had ticked up a notch since the second our fingers met still hadn't gone down. Delayed reaction, I suppose. I didn't like the pity, but his touch? I definitely didn't mind that.

"When I first started my career"—Emry pulled his arm back,

jolting my attention back to his words while missing his touch straight away—"I was a total nobody. I mean, I'd never even had a piano lesson in my life, and I was auditioning for big shows."

I smiled. Something about the idea of Emry not cowering in the face of improbable odds filled me with a warm feeling. He was so strong. Fearless. Even with the odds stacked against him, he persevered. So, in other words, he was the exact opposite of me.

"But I fought my way to get a foot in the door. I played crappy shows in tiny venues. Everyone thinks classical music is all about getting to perform at these beautiful venues like Carnegie Hall, the Sydney Opera House, or the Wiener Musikverein in Vienna. But trust me, there are plenty of crappy places to play at, too. And I've played 'em all, Miguel. Success takes time. It doesn't happen overnight. As the expression goes, Beyoncé wasn't built in a day."

We looked at each other and shared the smile that burgeoned between us.

"The key is to keep going. Never look back, only ahead. What's done is done. It can't be changed. The only thing you can do is focus on the future."

Good advice. And not just for my career, but for life in general.

I mulled his words in my mind throughout the rest of the evening. The meal was everything I'd heard guests raving about and more. But it was the company that was truly spectacular. As I studied him during the course of our conversation, I noticed how free he was.

When he spoke, he did it with his whole body, his arms talking just as much as his mouth.

When he smiled, it reached his eyes and his whole face permeated with a wondrous glow.

And his clothes? Man, did the guy have style. I'd never seen a shirt like what he was wearing before. It looked expensive and like it had been made for him. Heck, maybe it had been. It was a black, white, and yellow dual-print buttoned shirt. On the left side, it sported a Baroque print, and as I looked a little closer, the other side had a signature print on it. With a little—and hopefully discreet—squint, I made out the name: Versace. Of course. But he could've been wearing something from the bargain bin at Walmart and still looked stellar.

"Thank you, Emry," I said as we wrapped up our dinner. I gestured for him to go ahead of me as we left the restaurant and headed down the path back to the main resort area. "That was a wonderful meal, and..."

Emry stopped walking and turned to face me, causing me to stop mid-sentence, the words left hanging in the space between us. I didn't know if it was the warm, salty evening air, or the sweet scent of tropical flowers that encased us, or the fact that looking into Emry's eyes took that small feeling of being unburdened and turned it into something even better.

I took a half step in toward him. "...and I really enjoyed your company. I mean it."

With his eyes trained on me, he replied, "I really enjoyed spending time with you, too."

The faint sounds of waves crashing in the distance and my heartbeat rattling in my ears were the only sounds I could hear.

What was happening?

What was about to happen?

Desire welled within me and just as our chests pulled closer, like we were magnets being drawn to each other, a loud voice hammered into our little cocoon, splintering the moment before anything more came of it.

"Coming through."

A party of six diners were making their way toward the restaurant and we were standing right in the middle of the path. We scuttled over to the side, letting them pass. Once they did, whatever moment we'd been sharing had passed, too. Just my luck.

"Hey, wanna grab a drink?" I suggested, not ready for the night to be over.

Even as the dimly lit path cast shadows on our faces, I could clearly make out the *are you serious* look Emry was throwing me.

"I said *drink*. As in singular. Don't you worry. I've learned my lesson after last night."

With an unexpectedly loud and joyous giggle, Emry agreed. "Sure. Let's do it."

And with that, we headed to the onsite bar.

17

EMRY

The bar was packed. No, wait, that was putting it mildly. It was crammed tighter than the two cocks Hawk and I had stuffed into Brock's very willing—and accommodating—ass two days earlier.

It was located right above the main lobby, the elevation allowing for an awesome view of the entire resort, right out into the pitch-black night of ocean and sky. As we made our way inside, I was struck by all the times I'd been here with Hawk and with other friends. Coming here with Miguel felt different. It almost had a date-night feel to it. Almost.

"Whoa." The word escaped me before I'd even realized I'd uttered it.

Miguel was pressed so close next to me our faces were a mere inch or two from touching. Someone stumbled by us drunkenly and with an unexpected shove, I ended up right in Miguel's face. I felt the warm grip of his fingers on my shoulders as he steadied me.

He inclined his head to look at me. "You okay?"

"Yeah," I replied, struck by the fact that Miguel was touching me...and I kinda liked it.

"Good." Miguel flashed the guy who had bumped into me a dirty look, but it was no use. He was already off wobbling into another group of guys who had entered behind us. At least the guy had the good sense to know he'd had enough and was heading back to his room.

"Follow me." Miguel released me and swiped his hand through his hair. He turned and I followed him, just like I'd let him lead me here. And just like before, my poor brain scrambled to make sense of *why* I was following him, and *what* I was wanting to get out of this experience.

The place was so busy that we weren't walking as much as shuffling, inching our way around the edge of the massive dance floor and through the sweaty churn of dancing bodies. The tribal-sound dance music was pumping loudly, the beat vibrating through my chest, and green laser beams shot out across the space, making my mind spin...even more than it already was.

"You might need to hang on." A devilish smile crossed his lips.

Hang on? What did he mean by that? I was confused until I saw Miguel's fingers patting down against his shoulders. Oh. Right. Hang on...*to him*. I could—I could do that.

I inhaled sharply as I lifted my arms, my hands docking in the groove of his shoulder blades. And that's how we muddled our way to the bar on the other side of the dance floor. Once there, the crowd thinned a little, the dance floor being the main attraction. With my hands still firmly gripping onto Miguel—they'd shifted slightly and were now cupping the smooth skin at the base of his neck—I could feel the pull of the dancefloor calling.

This getaway had taken a few unexpected twists and turns. Normally, I came to Elysian with Hawk to switch my brain off. I'd lounge by the pool, get some amazing treatments at the day spa, gorge on delicious food, and score some casual sex. All easy and fun and physical things that didn't require a lot of brainpower.

Running into Miguel, as well as the lingering stench from the rude asshole yesterday, had changed all that. But there was one way I could reset my body, mind, and spirit: dancing.

Before I could get Miguel's attention to see if he wanted to join me, I spotted a group of familiar faces sitting at the bar. Hawk, Leo, and a few of the guys I recognized from Miguel's comedy routine last night were hanging out.

As soon as Hawk's eyes found me, he tore out of his seat and thundered over to me. "Hey," he growled as he brushed past Miguel. I let go of Miguel and he turned around to face the both of us.

"I'm Miguel, the world's worst comedian," he said to Hawk, offering him a warm smile and a handshake.

"Nice to meet you."

They shook hands. To anyone else, the exchange would have seemed pleasant. Okay, maybe that was too strong a word. Let's go with civil. But to me, knowing Hawk like I did, I could tell he was on edge. He didn't like Miguel. He was just too nice to ever be rude to the guy's face about it.

"Can I get you guys a drink?" Miguel asked us both.

"I'm good," Hawk replied instantly, a scowl rising across his features as he lifted his beer bottle.

"Sure," I said brightly. "I might have a Fuck Me Like You Know My Name, please."

"Cool. I'll be right back."

"Don't hurry," I heard Hawk mutter into his beer.

"Hey, are you okay?" I chewed down on my bottom lip. I knew that he was just being testy because he was being protective of me. While I appreciated that, I also wanted him to know that Miguel was a decent guy. More importantly, I was an adult and didn't need to be looked after or coddled.

"Just horny," Hawk said somewhat dismissively, not looking at me but scanning the packed dance floor.

I didn't believe that was all that was going on. I decided to press one last time. "You sure?" I placed my hand on his shoulder and was struck how it didn't produce the same response as I'd felt when I touched Miguel in pretty much the exact same spot.

"Yep." He finally turned to face me, his eyebrows sky high and a distractingly weird smile painted on his face. "Wanna do a whore lap?"

It took me a moment to recalibrate from his deflection. It was like we were having two different conversations. "I can't, Hawk." I felt my chest tightening, sensing something brewing between us.

"Why not?" he demanded, showering me with a look that was a much lighter shade than what he'd subjected Miguel to but was still in the same family of mildly pissy and annoyed.

"Well, for starters"—I scrubbed the back of my neck—"I'm here hanging out with..." I trailed off but dipped my head in the direction of the bar. I could see Miguel leaning over, placing his order with the bartender. His dark pants clung tight to his legs, and the slight bend forward really highlighted just how solid his ass was.

"Miguel." The way Hawk practically spat his name out stopped my mind mid-track.

I returned my focus to my ever increasingly irritated, bristling friend. "Yes, Hawk." I placed a hand on my hip. Hawk might have been bigger and more physically imposing than me, but I was no pushover, and frankly, this whole watchful big brother act was starting to get on my nerves.

I decided to take my defiance up a smidge. "I'm here hanging out with *Miguelllll*." I deliberately drawled out his name. The muscle in Hawk's jaw seemed to be enjoying the music. It was beating pretty much in time to it.

"Fine, then. Enjoy your evening."

"Fine, then. I will."

As soon as Hawk stormed off, I couldn't help but feel bad. But whatever. I was sure we would talk about it tomorrow and have everything resolved by the time he saved us our usual two deckchairs by the pool.

"Hey, where did your friend go?" Miguel returned, handing me my drink.

"To find a fuck," I said a little too bluntly, judging by the surprised expression on Miguel's face.

"Is there something going on with you two?"

I took a hearty swallow of my drink. "Nope, we're just friends."

Miguel didn't look like he was buying it, but I didn't feel like getting into the elaborate story of how we became dick twins. In fact, I was getting kinda fed up with the whole talking and thinking thing, too.

I turned to him, my cheeks pulling into an optimistic smile. "Do you like having fun?"

He squinted suspiciously. "Uh, sure. I like fun."

"Cool." I grabbed his drink out of his hand and placed it on the small table a few feet away from us, along with my own. "Let's go dance."

I was just about to head toward the dance floor when I noticed Miguel hadn't moved.

"Uhhh..." The soft noise dropped from his lips, but despite the music blaring, I heard it clear as day.

I stepped back. "What's the matter, Miguel?"

He lowered his eyes to the ground. "I can't dance."

"What, no. That's impossible." I started bopping to the beat, shimmying my shoulders around playfully. That seemed to relax him a little. It even drew a slight smile around the corners of his mouth. "Everyone can dance, Miguel. There's no right or wrong way."

He stiffened again. "No, like, I'm really bad. Whatever dance gene gay guys are blessed with must've skipped me. I don't have two left feet, Emry. I have three, and I stumble over all three of them. I'm like Bambi on ice in the middle of a hurricane."

Normally, I wouldn't have pushed. Normally, I would've said something like, *I'll go and dance and we can catch up later*. But this wasn't a normal situation.

I smiled as I detected a hint of something underpinning this entire exchange between us. Something unexpected.

Power.

It was a subtle change, like turning on dimmable lights real slow until you suddenly realize, *Oh, someone's turned the lights on*.

Someone had turned the lights on.

Me.

The switch was in my hands, and I was turning it to the precise setting that I wanted. And what I wanted was to dance with Miguel.

"Trust me, it'll be fun."

His lips remained pressed. Shame, since they were so full and luscious. I moved in even closer. "I mean, come on, Miguel. Your dancing can't be any worse than your comedy, right?"

To be clear, I was kidding, I was kidding, I was kidding. But fuck, would he get that? I wasn't known for my humor. Killer fashion sense and all-around fierceness? Yes. Telling the funnies? Not so much.

His silence stunned me, and my heart clamped tight in my chest. And then the most amazing thing happened. Miguel's face went from stone cold and borderline pained to breaking out into the most wonderful smile. It loosened his jaw, reached his eyes, and erased all the wrinkles that had formed on his forehead. The transformation left him positively glowing, and me struggling to breathe.

"All right then, Emry Black"—a playfulness threaded through his tone as his eyes raked over me—"let's go and have some fun."

With a happy nod, I took hold of his hand, and this time, I was the one leading and Miguel was the one half a step behind me.

Destination: dance floor. Fun...here we come!

18

MIGUEL

One of all my all-time favorite episodes of Seinfeld was *The Little Kicks*. That was the one where Elaine did some, uh, interesting dancing. Okay, *interesting* was the wrong word. More like the most cringe-inducing, *please take my eyes out because this is so bad* type of dancing.

Yeah, well, if Elaine Benis were dancing next to me, she'd look like a ballerina. At least Elaine moved to the music. I couldn't. I didn't know how to get my feet to move. Forward? Back? Side to side? What was the deal here?

I desperately tried to take in what the guys around us were doing, but between the jungle beats deafening me, and the lasers temporarily blinding me every few seconds (note to self: do not look directly into them), I was a mess.

Emry, on the other hand, was tearing up the dance floor with sleek moves and sassy facial expressions flowing so effortlessly from him. Everyone around us disappeared as I soaked him in, studying every part of him like I was cramming for an exam I desperately needed to pass.

A *so thin it was almost sheer* layer of sweat precipitated on his face, elevating his delicate features with a luminous quality. His hair continued to impressively defy gravity, but it had loosened from its perfectly styled hold into something more relaxed, as Emry bounced and bopped all around me.

I wished that smiling counted as dancing because man, I would've been the best dancer on that dancefloor.

I mean, we'd almost kissed, right? I hadn't imagined that as we were walking from the restaurant. If it hadn't been for that group of guys barging through, would I have actually gone through with kissing Emry?

Thankfully, his friend who hated me, and wasn't shy about it, had taken off by the time I came back from the bar with drinks. So now it was just me and Emry and one hundred and forty beats per minute ricocheting through my body and still—*still*—my body was incapable of eliciting any more movement out of me than a wide grin.

"You're doing great," Emry's voice sang out at me from my left, but when I turned to look, there was no sign of him. I swiveled around to my right and there he was, a few feet in front of me, completely in his own world, losing himself to the music.

Excitement thrummed in my chest the longer I looked at him. He'd lied, of course. I was doing terribly. I was surprised the staff hadn't attempted to pick me up and remove me, mistaking me for a store mannequin that someone had placed in the middle of the floor on a lark.

I couldn't be sure what was happening here, but I was feeling all sorts of weird sensations. Was it the aftermath of finally apologizing to Emry after all these years? Was it seeing the man he had grown into, one who was successful and free and so confident in who he was? Or was it that I'd opened up to him about my dreams, as silly and unlikely as they now were?

I had no idea, but being so in my head about it produced an unlikely reaction in my body. It actually started to move on its own accord. Now, I had zero idea of whether my movements were in any way, shape, or form coordinated to match the beat. That was some next-level shit way beyond my current abilities. For me, this slight rocking from side to side, with an occasional knee dip and chest twist, *this* was me dancing.

"I love this DJ," Emry shouted into my ear. I heard his words, but I felt the touch of his hand against my back even more. He was looking euphoric, the smile so wide it threatened to overtake the lower half of his face, his whole body sparkling and so, so alive. I'd been mistaken earlier when I assumed he was lost in the music. He wasn't losing himself. He was reconnecting to another part, a deeper part of who he was.

I could see it in the wild abandon that radiated from him—his limbs becoming extensions of the rhythm, his body being molded into movement by the beat. It inspired me. I kicked it up a notch.

Up until now, I'd given him space. Technically, Emry was tearing up the floor with such ferocity that half the time I couldn't even tell where he was. He was moving and dipping and sliding all over the place. The sweet scent of his aftershave rolled over me, letting me know he was always near.

I took a few shaky steps toward him. He responded immediately. Through flashes of green laser lights, we latched on to each other's gaze. Shadows and light trickled magically across our bodies, wrapping around us, encasing us together like ribbon wrapped around a gift.

He dipped his shoulder and with a seductive sway, he was in my space, right in front of me. I felt his warm breath hit my neck as his hazel eyes flicked me a devious look. I couldn't be sure, though. What if I was only imagining it? But if I was, why were Emry's eyes now fixated on my lips?

Desire sparked in my bloodstream, charting its way throughout my body, stomping to glorious victory as it reached my cock, thickening it, hardening it, until the pressure felt like too much to bear.

The beat muddied into a pulsing background sound and without warning, the lights faded to black and the dance floor became deserted. There was no one else here. Nothing else mattered.

A wanting so strong it bordered on delirium began to spike through my body as Emry's hands found their new home around my neck. I trailed the back of my index finger along the ridge of his cheekbone.

There was just silence and air around us, until one, then two, and then a whole bunch more of them fell down. The sky tore open and bright yellow sparks buzzed around us. Fireflies.

I looped my hands around Emry's tiny waist. God, it was so small my fingers were practically touching. He smiled at the touch, letting me know he liked being held. I wanted nothing more than to lean in and kiss him so that I could hold on to that smile forever.

But I pushed that burning need down. Not because I didn't want to kiss Emry, but because I wanted Emry to kiss me first. I couldn't explain why, but it felt like the right thing to do.

Emry's fingertips pressed into the back of my neck. The feel of his fingers on my skin set off a construction zone in my chest, one that involved my heart pounding and jackhammering away like crazy. The beats of the music had been replaced by my own internal staccato orchestra.

Emry's head angled up as he pulled me in, his mouth curved into a devilish smirk.

"Are you trying to seduce me, Emry?" I kept my voice as steady as I could, but it was a betrayal of all the fireworks and energy whirring inside of me.

"No. Not trying."

And with that, he took my mouth in a way that knocked me off my feet. It was hard, ruthless and completely unapologetic. His tongue surged past my lips, storming into my mouth like it owned the damn place.

With my hands around his waist, I maneuvered him until there wasn't a gap of air between our bodies. His hands roamed up and down my back as he dominated my tongue and I blissfully surrendered to him.

Emry continued to manhandle my mouth like a boss as my hands glided up his lithe, smooth body, eventually raking them through his hair. If he was destroying my mouth, I at least wanted to mess up his normally perfectly coiffed hair a bit, too. With a growl escaping from the edge of his lips, Emry matched my movement, dragging his fingernails against my scalp.

"You like that?" he purred low and deep, and fuck if it wasn't the hottest thing I'd ever heard. Completely unexpected, too—in the best way possible. *Who was this guy?* I wondered with my head tilted up, succumbing to Emry's commanding hold.

"Yeah."

It was little more than a gargle—and most likely barely

decipherable—but it was all the permission Emry needed to bite into the column of my throat. The sweet strangle I felt as he nibbled my skin was out of this world.

I stumbled and fell against him. His hands pressed against my chest, steadying me, but he wasn't done kissing me. Not by a long shot. And as he stormed my mouth again, that's when it happened. A lifting, my feet levitating off the floor, hovering in the air as Emry rose with me. I cupped his face, clinging to him as if my life depended on it.

And as we floated, our tongues a swirling mess of pure wet wanting, it dawned on me that the weird sensation I'd been experiencing came down to one thing, or rather, one person: Emry Black.

I opened my eyes and the sight of his face pressed close to mine, his own lids shut but fluttering, did something to me. I felt something move inside of me, as if I were being rearranged from the inside out, like Cavity Sam in the board game Operation.

I tore away from Emry's clamped lips, licking little kisses up and down his cheeks, across his jaw and as he canted his head upward, under his chin, too.

And that's when I saw it. A nick. Small. Probably no more than an inch. Sure, it could've been from shaving, but no other part of his skin was marked like this. No, this blotch was different. And while his makeup had covered it before, there was no missing it now. Or mistaking its origin. Someone had done this to him.

Emry's fingers continued tousling my hair as he brushed our lips together. A single tear rolled down my cheek. What felt like a lifetime of hidden pain, shame, and guilt careened into me all at once.

A small, sinister voice inside my head instructed me to remember this, to lock every tiny detail of this moment into my memory vault. The desire that had raced through my veins was overtaken by a corpulent guilt rolling in my gut as I tried to reconcile this kiss—this truly magical moment—with the past, and what I had done to him.

Barbed wire pierced into my brain as I tried to desperately swim against the changing tide of thoughts pummeling me. But there was no use in fighting it. There was a good chance—no, wait, there was one hundred percent certainty that by the time the moon gave way to the sun, this moment would be nothing more than a memory. I broke the kiss and looked at my feet.

They were planted firmly on the dance floor.

SUNDAY

19

EMRY

I jackknifed myself awake, bursting out of the weirdest dream I'd had in a long time. I was on a dance floor, making out with Miguel.

Letting out a thunderous yawn, I slid the back of my index finger against my swollen top lip. That's when it hit me. It hadn't been a dream. The taste of Miguel lingered on me. I fell back stiffly, like a tree being lobbed by its base, my head bouncing around on my fluffy pillow as the events of last night tumbled around in my mind.

Needing to work my way up to thoughts of kissing Miguel, I focused on something less heavy and way, way more bad: the poor guy's dancing skills. Although *skills* really was an overreach. Miguel's dance moves would have relieved every single dad and uncle in the country who was worried his dance moves were bad because Miguel's were on a level of tragic I had never seen before.

Or at least, that's how they started as he managed to stay oddly still. His arms swinging around his body was basically his only movement. But then something changed. I didn't know how or why, but he loosened up. A lot. Still not great as far as dancing went, but at least it looked like he was at least hearing the same music I was bouncing along to.

I had needed that release so badly—to bump, grind, and thrust my way in a sea of sweaty bodies, letting go of all the pent-up energy that had been building up inside of me.

Another yawn interrupted my stupid grinning and sent my thoughts traveling back to the thing that had caused me to wake up so abruptly this morning: Miguel's mouth.

Up until last night, my mind had been on everything but Miguel's sweet-tasting lips. I'd been preoccupied with either keeping thoughts of my past locked up tight in that little box I never allowed myself to even go near or consoling the guy about his failed performance. Now, his lips had rammed their way so deep into my head that they were all I could obsess over.

With a sudden gust of energy, I swept the cover off me and strode over to the full-length window, drawing the curtains apart.

The sun blazed through, flooding the room as the warmth hit my naked body.

Miguel had made an abrupt exit last night after we finished dancing. He'd mumbled something about having an early start today and then he was gone. I wasn't able to find Hawk or Leo, so I called it a night, too.

Why was I so fixated on Miguel's lips? I mean, yes, they tasted amazing. And yes, they drew out a response in me that might have bordered on ravenous. And boy, was the guy a good kisser, or what. But what in the name of Destiny's Child had come over me last night to practically maul him like that?

Yes, I knew what he'd done to me in the past was all sorts of shitty and wrong. Miguel was my high school bully and yet, I wasn't mad or hurt or pissed off at him about it. In fact, I didn't feel anything. See, that was the beauty of neatly tying emotions up and locking them away. They couldn't come back to taunt or torment you.

And he apologized for it, even acknowledging that one apology was only a starting point. He also mentioned that he should've been down on his knees begging me for forgiveness. I didn't know about that, although the thought of Miguel on his knees with those dusky eyes blinking up at me...now, *that* wasn't an entirely unpleasant thought.

I felt a sticky coldness in my groin. I looked down and my fully erect, leaking cock was pressed against the window. I groaned. Being hard about all of this only made my thoughts turn to an even bigger pile of sludge than they were already in.

Whatever had swept over us last night surely had to be a one-time thing, right?

I took half a step back, keeping my gaze on the never-ending ocean in front of me. It was a peculiar feeling. I could still feel Miguel's taste, his scent, his touch, on me. At the same time, I felt a new feeling, a lightness, similar to the weightlessness I'd felt after getting struck by lightning.

Normally, I liked not having full access to my emotions. It made it easier to hide them away if I just labeled them as unwanted, without digging my nose around to determine what emotions they actually were. What was the point of that? Shit was shit. I didn't need to go digging any further into it than that.

But this morning, a tiny crack appeared in the veneer I'd built around myself. Small, almost imperceptible, but definitely there.

It was a feeling that I couldn't manage to wash off as I showered or shake off me as I got dressed. It was a Sunday, so I decided to go with my Sunday kaftan. Just as fabulous as all the others, but in more subdued hues of tangerine and mustard.

As I wandered into the bathroom to get myself ready, my cell phone buzzed. Hawk was texting to let me know he'd secured our spots by the pool for the day. I replied, letting him know I'd join him in a few minutes.

After I'd showered, brushed my teeth, and applied my foundation, I gave myself an approving nod in the mirror. Gathering my essentials, I scooped up my bag and made my way to Hawk for what would be our last day of poolside hangs before heading back home.

The reality of that thought landed in my chest with a sinking thud. We'd be checking out tomorrow. Which meant that I wouldn't see Miguel again, at least not until I returned, which could be in a few months. I held back a deep sigh, surprised at how affected the idea of not seeing Miguel made me. I was actually saddened by the idea.

After doing my part to contribute to the thinning of the ozone layer, I took my Issey-spritzed self to the pool. As I closed the door and turned to leave, I ran smack bang into Miguel. "Oh, hey."

He was wearing the resort's all-black housekeeping uniform, the name Elysian embroidered in bright blue across the right pec of his tight-fitting polo. "Hey," he stuttered back.

Good to know I wasn't the only one feeling all sorts of things about what had happened last night. Although I couldn't help but wonder what he was making of all of this.

"Well, uh, this is weird," I said, wishing I'd sewn pockets into my kaftan so I could jam my hands into them. Instead, I wriggled my shoulders, adjusting the bag strap to sit more comfortably.

"Agreed." He scratched the side of his face. "Awkward on a scale not yet invented."

"Yep," I muttered back to him.

Wow...less than eight hours ago, we were mouth fucking like our lives depended on it. Now, exchanging more than a few syllables felt like a herculean effort.

We shifted out of the way of a couple who passed us by and exchanged a friendly "Hello" with them.

I noticed Miguel was carrying a bucket filled with a paper roll and a few bottles of what I assumed were cleaning supplies. Hmm, I thought he was the head of housekeeping. Weird, that he'd be cleaning rooms himself. "Are you short-staffed today?" I asked lamely, gesturing toward the bucket.

"No, why?"

"Um, no reason."

Somebody shoot me, please. I felt like a doddering old fool who had lost his ability to have a normal conversation with someone.

Except Miguel wasn't just someone. And as prepared as I was to unpin him from the former bully column, I was left with one big, unanswered question: just where did I pin him to next?

Under me with my cock sliding into that meaty ass of his.

Oh to the M to the G. Seriously, what was wrong with me?

I bit the inside of my cheek, praying I wasn't blushing like an idiot at my dirty thoughts, or that Miguel didn't have secret psychic powers so that he couldn't ascertain that they were all about him. Meanwhile, the silence between us stumbled on, with seemingly no end in sight.

Finally, Miguel broke it. "Don't suppose you've got any housekeeping uniform fantasies you want to live out?" Before I could even smile at his sunny remark, he winced and slapped the side of his face. "Shit, sorry. That was almost as bad as my act the other night."

"Actually, it was kinda funny. And by the way, Miguel, please stop beating yourself up over that. What's done is done."

I was referring to his act, but the double meaning of my words struck us both at around the same time.

Another couple squeezed past us, causing Miguel to shuffle over closer to me again. "Listen, Emry. I know you're leaving tomorrow, and Monday mornings are like a hurricane around here, so we won't really get a chance to talk."

My breath hitched in my throat as I realized what he was about to say. I wasn't ready for us to say goodbye—at least, not just yet. This was going to be the last time we saw each other and I found myself strangely unprepared.

"But," he continued, "I'd really like to see you again. Would you be up for having dinner with me tonight?"

I blew out the breath that had frozen halfway down my throat and nodded. "Sure, Miguel. I'd love that."

He smoothed his free hand through his hair. He looked...relieved? Did he really think I would say no to seeing him again? As he made his way past me, I twisted and called out, "Hey, where are we going? What should I wear?"

Miguel turned around but kept pacing backward, his face suddenly illuminated by the most dazzling smile I'd ever seen on him. "Wear whatever you want, Emry. You can wear a paper bag and socks with sandals—you'll still be the most beautiful guy in the world."

20

MIGUEL

Thankfully, Emry didn't take me up on my socks and sandals joke challenge. Instead, when I opened the door to my apartment, he was wearing dark jeans and a navy blue button-up shirt that could've been made of silk, given the way it glimmered whenever he moved. The sight was truly spectacular.

"Come in." I waved him in, and as I did, I noticed that my hand was trembling. I placed it against the door as he walked past me, hoping he didn't notice that, or the fact that I was breathing in his intoxicating aftershave that filled the air around us.

My place wasn't anything big or fancy, just a neat two bedroom condo in a newly built complex in Key West. I'd only moved in a few months earlier, and I really liked living here. As I considered all the places I could take Emry out to dinner, it struck me that the best place of all was a lot closer than I had thought. And as a bonus, I'd never been there, either.

"So, where are we going?" Emry asked as we stepped into the living room. If he was nervous, he sure didn't show it. "I hope what I'm wearing will be all right."

I gently grazed his back as I moved past him, flashing him a knowing smile. If I didn't know any better, I'd say he was fishing for a compliment. Not that I minded. If that's what he was doing, then call me Fisherman Miguel.

"You look amazing, Emry."

I opened the oven and pulled out a tray using my *Latin American Boys Do It Better* tea towel. The dish had been warming for the last half an hour or so. I felt Emry's breath heating the back of my neck as he peered over my left shoulder.

"It smells amazing. What's that?"

I turned to my left and there was less than a shoulder blade's distance between my mouth and Emry's. Our noses were so close they were almost touching each other. His eyes flared and my pulse rate shot up.

Without breaking eye contact, I kicked the oven door shut and placed the tray onto the countertop, freeing up my hands. They had much more important things they could be holding. Like Emry's beautiful face.

I turned around so that we were standing face to face. I was only a little taller than Emry, but I loved the angle his face created as he tipped his head in my direction. I glossed my tongue over my parched bottom lip, feeling unsure of myself. Out of my depth. I'd gotten as far as I could go, but how could I take it to the next—

Emry's lips brushing against mine kicked all doubts, fears, and coherent thinking outta my mind. Thank god. His fingers found the place they seemed to like so much at the back of my neck, as he pulled me into him. He didn't need to pull that hard. I was more than willing to go wherever he wanted me to.

His fingers tangled in my hair, and with a forceful tug, he tipped my head back, exposing my neck for him to devour. Which he did. Good thing I'd prepared a lot of food because this boy was hungry. Filthy slurping sounds filled the air in my tiny kitchen and sent something warm and fierce and delicious traveling up my spine. Emry was ravaging my throat and damn, I was living for it.

After a while, he looked up at me with a heat swirling in his eyes, making me think I was going to topple over. Hazel had been replaced with the color of a deep, wanting desire. Feelings that I had for him, too, but...what the fuck? How was this happening? Why on earth would a guy like Emry be interested in a loser like me?

"Eat," I gulped out. "We should eat."

A smile teased the corners of his mouth. "I thought that's what I was doing."

"I meant food." A magma red blush oozed up my neck at my completely unnecessary clarification.

Emry took a step back. "Sorry, I didn't mean to be coming on so strong." He shook his head, like he was waking up from some sort of stupor. "I—I don't know what came over me, actually."

"You don't have to apologize," I said hastily. "I just think we should talk. And eat. And talk while we eat."

Emry looked at me and we both giggled. Nervously. Stupidly. Like two high school kids on a date.

"So, you made food?" Emry eyed the covered tray on the counter.

"Yeah. Nothing fancy. Just a few traditional Salvadorian foods. I thought it might be interesting."

"You thought right. I like trying new things."

I pushed the double meaning away as I picked up the tray. "There's a bottle of wine by the sink and a small basket. Would you mind getting them, please?"

"Sure thing."

With supplies in hand, I headed toward the front door.

"Uh, where are we going?"

"You'll see," I replied over my shoulder. I smiled as Emry scrunched up his face in confusion, but that's not what made me so happy. It was that he was so close behind me. Again.

Less than a minute later, we arrived on the rooftop deck of my building. Residents could book this place out and use it to have a meal or hang out with friends. There was a small grill, a dining table, and a few outdoor couches scattered around the place.

My building wasn't in the fancy part of the city, but since we were back a little way from the action and on what was essentially the fourth floor, we had a great view of Key West and the ocean beyond it. "This is really nice," Emry observed as he took in the setting sun.

"I've never had Salvadorian food before. You'll have to tell me what everything is."

I smiled as I plated the food I'd prepared. "It's not much. I made pupusas. That's like the national dish. It's hand-made corn tortillas stuffed with various fillings such as beans, pork and cheese."

Emry rubbed his hands together. "Ooh, sounds yummy."

"There's also tamales, chicken pasteles which are fried dough patties mixed with vegetables, and for dessert, a traditional cake called quesadilla salvadorena."

"Wow, I'm impressed."

"It's nothing," I brushed his comment aside as I laid out the various dips and sauces in front of us. "Dig in."

I loved watching Emry's face as he ate the food, his eyes going wide as he experienced the new flavors for the first time. The evening was going well, but I couldn't ignore the elephant in the room. And no, I wasn't talking about the fact that kissing Emry was the most fun I'd had in years. Something else had been troubling me.

As someone who was an expert at self-punishment, it struck me that Emry was acting cool with us hanging out. Don't get me wrong. That was great and I loved spending time with him, but where was the anger? The resentment? And more importantly, the need to get it out of him?

Emry was a nice guy, but he had every right to yell at me for what I had done to him. Where was that in all of this? I'd meant it when I'd said my apology was only the beginning, a small step on a much longer journey toward really owning what I'd done and making up for it.

After a lull in the conversation, I decided to just come right out with it. "Emry, I have to ask, aren't you mad at me?"

Emry's eyes widened, then narrowed. His lips twitched, as if the words were trying to push their way out of his mouth but he wasn't quite ready to let them out. That was exactly what I wanted for him to do, though. Whatever it was—no matter how bad or ugly a verbal spray it would be—I wanted it. I had it coming. I *deserved* it. Even if I had to coax it out of him because he was too nice a guy to willingly do it himself.

After what felt like forever, he spoke. "I'm not mad, Miguel. I'm actually happy."

"Happy?" I didn't mean for the word to come out like a high-pitched squawk, but I couldn't help it. That was the last thing I'd expected to hear him say.

His voice was monotone. "I've dealt with that part of my life, Miguel. I've been to therapy. It didn't work for me."

"No?"

"No." He tapped his fingers against the edge of the table. "I know it works for other people and it's valuable for them, so no judgment at all. But for me, I ended up paying a shit ton of money only to confirm two things I already knew."

"And what were those two things?"

He replied instantly. "One, I had a shitty start to life. I was born in a small, bigoted town to parents who didn't understand me, and I got bullied every day in school."

Shame flooded me at the words, but I needed to hear this. I had inflicted so much pain onto him. I didn't think I'd ever be able to truly forgive myself for that. I didn't know anything about his home life, though.

"Your family, are you close?"

Emry's jaw tightened. "No."

"You have an older brother. Will, right?"

He gave a clipped nod. "Yeah. I don't have any contact with my parents or Will. They never accepted me—hell, they didn't even tolerate me."

I remembered Emry telling me how his parents had shipped him off to his uncle after his accident. My heart clenched at how horrible it must've been for him, to be treated so badly by the very people who were meant to love you unconditionally.

"I send them a Christmas card every year, with my contact details."

"You do?"

"Yeah." A small smile curled his lips. "It's what my uncle used to do. He never gave up hope that maybe one day, they'd crack. But my family is still closed off to me, and it's something I just have to accept."

There was no escaping the heaviness of his words. "You said there were two things," I reminded him. "That therapy taught you two things?"

"That's right." As he spoke, more color began filling in between the lines of his memories. "I realized that I loved myself then when I was going through all of that shit, and I love myself now."

A spark had been lit inside of him. I could feel it radiating off his skin. I was blown away. I had a feeling he was strong. People had always underestimated that about him—including me—but I could see that it was true. Even back in high school, he stayed true to who he was. He never changed or pretended to be someone he wasn't. Unlike me.

"How did you find that strength, Emry?"

He lifted a shoulder as he brought the wine to his lips. "I wish I knew 'cause then I could write a bestselling self-help book about it, get interviewed by Oprah, hang out with Barack and Michelle—they'd let me call them Barry and Mischy, of course—and then I could retire as a bestselling author by the age of twenty-five."

Loud peals of laughter engulfed the space between us. "Oh my god, you are incredible, Emry."

"And fucking fierce to boot," he added, quirking a perfectly manicured eyebrow at me.

"I one thousand percent agree."

Emry tapped his fingers on the table again. It looked like a reflexive action. Made sense since the guy was a world-class pianist after all. "I got sick of being labeled, you know?"

I gave a nod.

"I'm girly, so I must be weak. I'm femme, so I must be a slutty bottom. I got bullied as a kid, so I've got to have all these unresolved issues. All of that is complete and utter bullshit. I know who I am."

The steely resolve that had settled over his expression made me believe every single word coming out of his mouth.

"Yes, I had it tough. But you know what got me through it? Realizing that others had it worse. Sure, my home life was brutal and Dad would often lay into me, but at least I had a roof over my head. Too many kids don't. They end up on the streets and believe me, that's much worse."

I exhaled, considering the terrible truth of that thought.

"Yes, I got bullied every single day at school and marked down the days until the end of term in my diary. But it didn't change me, or who I was, or what I wore, or even how I acted."

That part was so true. It didn't.

"And hell, I got struck by goddamn lightning. I could have *died*, Miguel. Instead, I got a gift. One that changed my life, got me the fuck out of Blessing, Texas, and has given me everything I have today."

Emry was on a roll. "I don't rehash the past. It was shit. I got over it. I look ahead to the future and focus on what I want to focus on. What I want to achieve. What's ahead of me." He looked me straight in the eye as he said that. Something about what he'd been saying—and the confident ferociousness in *how* he said it—ignited the evening air around us.

I squashed the lump in my throat or at least, tried giving it my best shot. "And what is it that you want right now?"

A blistering heat crackled between us. I hadn't meant for it to come out like a cheesy line from a '90s porno flick, but it did, and the energy continued veering into a place seething with forbidden danger.

Emry wiped his mouth with the napkin and stood up. My eyes bulged at the sight before me. He was sporting a hard-on that I was pretty certain could be seen from outer space.

"What I want"—Emry muttered low as his eyes traveled the length of my body—"is to fuck the living daylights out of you."

21

EMRY

Whoa. Girl. Whoa!

Since when did I talk like that?

Fuck the living daylights out of you?

I cleared my throat and just as I opened my mouth to do the most epic walkback of all time, Miguel shot to his feet so fast he tipped his chair over.

His tongue darted out, moistening his bottom lip. "Yeah? What exactly did you have in mind, Emry?"

Oh. So, he was...into it?

I had no idea what I had in mind, but I'd be very happy to start with his succulent lower lip that I wanted nothing more than to bite into.

"Get over here," I growled, channeling my inner Hawk without even realizing it. I didn't know what I was doing—or why—but it was working. Miguel breezed into me, his warm breath colliding with my neck.

His lashes fluttered expectantly. "Yes?"

Shit. Now he actually expected me to talk. My stupid mouth shot off before my brain had a chance to cut in. I froze, but I knew it wouldn't last long. The heat in Miguel's eyes was melting right through me. So I did the only thing that resembled something close to sanity. I tugged Miguel into me and devoured those lips in one long ravishing kiss.

Was it wrong of me to be kissing Miguel as an opportunity to buy some time here? Except...whoa...this time, it wasn't me kissing Miguel. He was kissing me right back, too. Not just matching my force, but returning it with something extra—a delicious hunger that told me he was one hundred percent into me.

His fingers threaded into my hair as his tongue whipped its way inside my mouth. It was his turn to explore me, and he took to it like an explorer discovering a new world. The kiss was ravenous as he swirled his tongue around, probing every corner of my mouth. And I stood there...and let him.

Okay, brain? Hello? Are you in there? Yes, I'm enjoying this moment immensely, but unless this kiss lasts until the end of time—side note: *not* such a bad thought—you and I are going to have to work together to come up with a game plan here. There's still the whole, you know, matter of the words that had flown out of my mouth we need to resolve.

What had gotten into me?

I laid the blame squarely on the broad shoulders of the guy currently plunging his tongue so hard into my mouth that he was able to do the one thing no one else had ever even come close to doing: breaking down the barricade I had built around my past.

In a way, he was one of the few people who could.

I'd essentially broken down my life into two parts: everything that happened until I left Blessing and my life since. Those two worlds never, ever overlapped. One was a happy world that I'd created, where I was the truest, freest, and most successful version of myself. The other was haunted by people, places, and experiences that I never wanted to return to.

Except now I was kissing one of those people from that other part of my life...and it wasn't the worst thing. Scary? Yes. But, bad? No. I'd been obsessing about Miguel ever since we kissed. How could I not? That kiss was everything, and Miguel was beautiful. But there was more going on here than just a physical attraction. Spending time with Miguel was unlocking parts of me I had kept hidden and locked away.

"So," Miguel whispered as he peppered my chin and neck with tender, featherlight kisses, "tell me more about how you want to fuck me."

Oh. Right. *That.*

Since thinking clearly wasn't working out that well for me, I tried a different tack—I went with my gut.

I pulled on his hair roughly, forcing his eyes to meet mine. He gawked at me. Was he surprised by my behavior? Turned on? Both?

In some ways, it was so unlike me. I never acted like this. Yet, it didn't feel unnatural, either. I wanted Miguel, and there was something more in my attraction to him that was bubbling just underneath the surface.

I broke the stare, quickly taking in the empty rooftop. The sun had set, but a dim orange light still permeated the evening glow. A few clouds teased the horizon. "I want you, Miguel."

"Same," he shot back instantly.

"Here."

His eyebrows lifted with interest. "Here?"

I leaned in, our foreheads touched. "I want to fuck you, right here and right now."

The filthy words whirred around in the air between us.

He pulled back slightly. A downturned smirk graced his lips. "It's right about now that I wish I'd packed condoms and lube, rather than plates and cutlery in that picnic basket."

"Have you got supplies in your apartment?"

He nodded.

"Good. Go get them."

With another nod, he raced off to get supplies, leaving me on the rooftop of an apartment building by myself and wondering— what the hell was I doing?

I walked over to the edge of the rooftop, inclined my head to the darkening sky, letting out a breath I felt like I'd been holding for most of my life. This was happening, and I wasn't just talking about having sex with Miguel. Well, I was, but it was more than that, too. Being with him meant that my two perfectly compartmentalized and distinctly separate worlds would collide. That was the real deal about what I was doing—and about to do —here.

Maybe that helped to explain why I was talking and acting in a way that I barely recognized. My composure, my carefully controlled everything; it was disintegrating into the gentle gusts of wind that were blowing around me. As I heard Miguel's footsteps returning, clouds began to move in, covering the early night sky with a dark fog.

Miguel reached me and brushed his lips against mine. I eased into the touch, the softness of his lips, the gracefulness of his fingers as they hooked under my shirt and grazed the sensitive skin around my hip bones.

A rapturous heat buzzed through me. God, I wanted him. I wanted *this*. The blistering look he shot me sparked something in me, something untapped, something I'd never felt in my life.

"Get down on your knees," I commanded, and without hesitation, Miguel obeyed and dropped to the ground. The sight of him, his dark curls framing his forehead, his deep eyes peering up at me, his mouth gently parted—*fuck*, it hit me harder than granite.

And then it dawned on me what was happening here—the emotions swirling around in my chest, the prickling of heat that ignited my nerve endings...

I was about to rage fuck my high school bully.

The even crazier thing was that he seemed totally down for it.

Miguel cupped the bulge in my pants and hungrily kneaded the swelling flesh between his fingers. My desperate need for him formed a lake of hot lava at the base of my spine. It oozed up my back as his hands caressed my cock through the material.

Miguel tugged at the button and zipper of my pants, making it clear he wanted some skin on skin action. I helped him out—it was never easy getting someone else's pants off while you were on your knees, and after all, politeness counts—but he was perfectly fine to yank my pants halfway down my thighs.

My freed cock met the cooling evening air, but it didn't have long to savor it. Miguel took me in his mouth with one smooth swoop. "Jesus," I cried, steadying myself by leaning on his shoulders. "That's so good." Seriously, it was. The guy had no gag reflex and seemingly, no need to warm up. He went from zero to deepthroating in under five seconds.

No complaints here, though, as he found a fast but steady

rhythm. Because of my size, most guys used their hands to complement their mouth action, but not Miguel. One of his hands was massaging my balls, while the other one was stroking my inner thigh. Fuck, how I loved that. It was an erogenous zone most guys overlooked, but not Miguel. He circled his fingers over the slightly hairy thigh, sending shivers up and down my spine.

I lost track of time, surrendering to the sweet sensation Miguel was producing within me, but at some point, a light drizzle had started to fall. I only noticed it when Miguel looked up, and I saw the drops falling onto his face, making his long lashes quiver.

Miguel gripped the base of my cock and pulled off of me. "Are you okay to continue?" he asked.

I managed a nod and eked out a, "Yes," but his firm grip around me made even a simple task like that seem near impossible.

I cleared my throat and regained some composure. "What about you, Miguel?" He was the one on his knees, giving a blowjob in what was now becoming a sprinkle. I wanted to make sure he was comfortable. I cupped my hands around his jaw, signaling that I wanted him to come up.

He got to his feet and planted a soft, slightly wet kiss on my lips. "I'm good. I don't mind a little rain. But if there's lightning"— he wagged a finger between us—"then we go inside."

I tangled my fingers in his hair and smiled. "Afraid of a little lightning, are we?"

"I'm not. But what about you?" His voice was so deep and low it sounded like velvet, the genuine concern for me unmissable.

"Miguel," I muttered as I brought my lips tantalizingly close to his. "I've already been struck once. What are the odds I'd get hit by lightning again?"

He stared at me for a few beats, and I got lost in his long lashes and brooding eyes. He was trying to make sense of this just like I was. But maybe this was one of those things that couldn't be figured out. Not entirely. Not right now. And not with words.

Miguel seemed to be on the same wavelength as he pulled me

into him again. We kissed in the rain, deep and hard, as if we were trying to quench a bottomless thirst. My hands wrapped around his narrow waist as our tongues continued to tangle, the rain getting heavier by the second.

That's when it hit me. This time, the lightning wouldn't strike me from above. This time, I was holding it right in my hands.

22

MIGUEL

I'm not gonna lie. Outdoor fucking in the rain is exactly as hot as it sounds. It was starting to come down harder now, but did I give a flying fuck? Uh, that would be a hell to the no. The only thing I cared about was kissing Emry with everything I had in me...and enjoying the way he was kissing me right back.

Now that we'd established we were okay to continue, my mind returned to what we'd been doing just before. This might sound weird, but I had a feeling Emry wasn't going to be a stereotypical twinky bottom. Don't know how I knew that, but I just felt it. I hadn't been expecting him to be quite as...authoritative as he was, though, but, um, yeah...literally zero fucking complaints about that. It aligned perfectly with what I liked.

But now, I was hungry for more, and I needed to take a chance to see whether Emry was ready to take it to the next level.

Our clothes were soaked, so I suggested, "Let's get undressed."

Emry nodded, and sure, while it may have been a romantic gesture to slowly undress each other while we stared deeply into each other's eyes, the fact was it was raining and we were both horny as fuck. Our clothes hit the floor in record time, but before I could sense the coolness sweeping over my skin, Emry tugged me into him, the roughness of the motion offset by the warmth of his chest and the thundering of his heart meeting mine.

I smoothed my hands down his chest and tilted my head, wanting to enjoy the view—and I didn't mean from the rooftop. His pristine hair was flattened by the rain, his eyes were wide and dreamy, and the tanned tips of his slender shoulders glistened with rain; he really was the most gorgeous creature I'd ever seen.

As much as I could've stared at him forever, there was another, more pressing matter at hand. With our gazes locked, I took a deep breath and said, "Emry, I want you to fuck me like you hate me."

His eyes shifted, scanning my face with a buzzing curiosity, and for a second, I panicked, thinking I'd royally misread the situation. That fear was allayed when he brushed a wet clump of hair off my forehead, leaned in and whispered, "You got it."

We made our way over to the ledge, making sure to take supplies with us. I turned away from Emry and leaned my arms against the railing, taking in the smattering of city lights in front of us. No one could see us directly, but we were still about to fuck on an open-air roof. This was totally the coolest sex thing I'd ever done.

I heard a few fumbled sounds behind me and then a cool wetness hit my ass. Emry's fingers landed in my ass crack and he was making his way to my entrance. I felt the slickness of his fingertips graze against my hole. The touch was slow and gentle and circular. I felt giddy already.

"I want you." I looked over my shoulder and the heat coming out of Emry's eyes floored me. I braced myself against the ledge as Emry slowly slid a finger into me.

"I want you, too," he whispered against the back of my neck. "I'm going to start slowly to get you warmed up, but then..."

He stopped talking, the fucking tease.

"Then what?" The need in my voice was thick.

"I'm going to fuck you like I hate you."

Hearing Emry repeat my own filthy words back to me got me *this close* to coming right there and then.

He meant what he'd said. He took his time prepping me. If I didn't know any better, I'd say he was enjoying it a little too much. Did he know he was subjecting me to the sweetest kind of torture? I kept my need in check and mouth shut. This was Emry's show. I wanted to see what he had in him, and I wanted to show him that I could go anywhere he wanted to take me.

After he'd fingered me with three fingers for a good while, he slowly pulled out. "Gimme a sec," he said, tearing the condom wrapper with his teeth.

I smiled, closed my eyes, and as I let out a deep breath, I felt the tip of Emry's cock press against me. "Are you ready?" he asked.

"Yes. I am," I shot back. I glanced over my shoulder. "Give it to me, Emry."

His name was barely off my lips when I felt a thundering force pierce into me. "Holy shit," I hissed, flinging my head back. Except it wasn't me doing it. It was Emry's fingers threaded through my hair, pulling me back as he bottomed out.

Heavy raindrops pelted my face as Emry thrust into me, his hips angled perfectly to drive in and out of me in long, furious strokes. He was right. He wasn't taking it easy on me at all. And I was living for it.

He let go of my hair and entwined his fingers around my throat, applying just enough pressure to let me know he was there. He pressed against my Adam's apple, and the slight hitch it caused in my breathing felt divine.

I was getting fucked in the rain on my rooftop, and I loved everything about this. How on earth did he know that this was what I loved so much? That I'd be into this? My deepest desire, the part of myself that I wanted so badly to explore but felt so ashamed of at the same time. It had always been my dirty little secret—my submissive sexual side. But with Emry, it didn't feel dirty or wrong or any of the other things I was afraid it would.

It actually felt really beautiful and pure.

Now I'm not going to say that the rain was symbolic of a cleansing or some shit like that, but the pounding I was getting, from both the sky above me and Emry behind me, not only felt good, it was releasing something within me.

And damn, it just felt soooo good.

I had a feeling Emry might've been a top, but I didn't think that he had this side to him as well. None of the guys I'd ever been with had been able to do what he was doing so effortlessly. I'd always felt so ashamed for liking rough, dominant sex. Most guys saw it depicted in porn and thought that's what it was.

Uh, no.

To me, this wasn't wrong or degrading. It was a hard thing to explain, but sex like this filled a part of me like nothing else could. And right now, as Emry dug his fingers into my neck and thrust into my body with such ferociousness, all I felt was electrified and beautiful and special.

I hoped he was feeling the same.

"You good back there?" I managed to grunt out. He was really fucking me hard now, the movement rocking through my entire body.

"I'm getting close," he panted.

"Good. Same."

Being dominated like this, surrendering to the strength of another man, was the most incredible feeling in the world. And as Emry bucked into me as his orgasm hit him, I closed my eyes and finished myself off, too.

Our bodies trembling, still connected, the rain really pouring down hard. It was the most exquisite, surreal feeling. I wished I could trap time and make it last forever.

But then, of course, stupid reality had to rear its ugly head. It started with Emry having to pull out of me, leaving behind an aching emptiness.

As I stood up and cracked my neck, our eyes met. His were dark, and I could see he was starting to lose himself in his thoughts. He needed something from me, but I didn't know what that was. I was still recovering from my own mind-destroying, soul-shuddering orgasm.

And then shit really got real when Emry chewed down on his lip as a pained expression overtook his face. "Well, I guess...I guess this is goodbye?"

TWO WEEKS LATER

23

EMRY

I shifted at the edge of the seat, straightening my spine ever so slightly as my fingers flew over the keys. I loved the feel and familiarity of the experience, almost more than the exquisite piece I was playing. There always came a moment, usually around this point, where the instrument, the music, and I connected and became one.

The Walt Disney Concert Hall in Los Angeles was packed to capacity on the last night of our limited eight-day run. As my fingers ran over the white and black Sitka spruce keys, I steadied my breathing. The epic, brooding buildup of Beethoven's Fifth Symphony was approaching, and I wanted to nail the crescendo that bridged the third and fourth movements.

The tonal switch from light to dark, soft to sweeping, was exciting to play. My fingers finished the punchy rhythms and probing legato, surrendering to a massive dominant chord blast of C major goodness. I didn't look up, but I could feel the audience lift with me as the crescendo took us all higher. I closed my eyes and felt the music envelop me in a gushing, warm embrace.

The last time someone had actually held me was Miguel, two weeks ago on his rooftop in Florida, and damn, if I didn't miss him. And as had been the case every single day since leaving Elysian, the second my thoughts turned to Miguel, they remained stuck on him.

I finished off the rest of the piece and half an hour later was back in my hotel room, my thoughts still fixed on him.

I should have been packing—I had an early flight back home the next day—but I was coming off a performance high and was way too distracted. Instead, I had a shower and slipped into the hotel's complimentary white robe and slippers, ordered room service, and did what I had been doing nonstop since returning from vacation: obsessing over Miguel.

That rooftop sex was emblazoned in my mind. It was the wildest, craziest thing I'd done, and believe me, in our time, Hawk and I had done some pretty epic sex stuff. But that was on a whole other level.

Even now, I still didn't know what had come over me, or Miguel, or both of us, as we connected in such a raw, honest, and tender way. And while it had been out of this world spectacular, I couldn't help but hope we'd get another chance to be together. Because if we did, I had something even hotter in mind for our follow-up round.

A knock on the door, followed by a muffled, "Room service," snapped me out of my daydream and alerted me to the fact that I was sporting a raging hard-on.

"Uh, you can leave it by the door, please."

I winced, knowing what a dick move that was. But too bad. There was no way I was opening the door to let room service see me with my cock protruding out of my robe. And as I scooped up the dessert tray left outside my door, I decided I'd make up for it with an extra large tip for housekeeping tomorrow morning. And of course, just the word *housekeeping* was enough to lead me straight back to my Miguel-inspired thought parade.

There were two main parts to how this went. First, I'd get all excited (sometimes, literally) thinking about Miguel. Yes, the sex part but other things as well. How it felt talking to him, the way his full lips would stretch out into the dazzling smile, the soul-level sincerity in his apology, making me believe it in my bones that he wasn't that same kid from high school anymore.

That part was good. The second part? It called for backup in the form of a large slice of baked New York cheesecake, with a side of whipped cream, a side of vanilla ice cream, and a side of seasonal berries, because health goals, right?

The second part was where shit went downhill. It all started with the question: but was any of it real? And then it kinda snowballed from there. Was it just a vacation thing, something to be relegated to a fun and exciting memory? Was it a one-time thing? It had to be, right?

What was he thinking and feeling about it? He worked at an all-male resort. Each week, he'd be able to sample from a veritable all-you-can-eat buffet of new guys. Working at Elysian, he probably got more ass than a proctologist. Why would he want to settle with just one guy?

I'll stop now, but take my word for it: *that* was just the tip of the iceberg of my thoughts descending into a never-ending hellish stream.

I kept plowing into the decadent dessert as I lay on my bed, some Netflix show playing silently on the flatscreen TV, hoping the combination of sugar, carbs, and fat would go some way to reining in the torrent of emotions that Miguel had unleashed in me. But yeah, I'd need more than dessert to help me get over this, mainly because...I didn't want to get over this.

Which was so stupid it made my head hurt with its sheer stupid-*ness*. Nothing to do with the heaped spoonful of ice cream I'd just shoved into my face. Damn, ice cream headaches were the worst. Once the stabbing sensation had passed, I vowed to eat slower and think slower, too.

I needed to get a handle on this. It'd been two weeks and I was just as caught up on Miguel as the day I'd left. Weren't these things meant to dissipate in time? The cold-shower-hit I'd been hoping reality would douse me with didn't eventuate, even though I knew this couldn't work.

For starters, we didn't even live in the same state. We hadn't spent long enough getting to know each other to even commit to a long-distance thing. I mean, one weekend. That wasn't long enough to start a relationship from...was it?

And that was probably the biggest issue of all. Aside from all the practical things like lack of a shared zip code, we didn't really know each other. We shared a past that by the looks of things, I was happy running away from and he seemed determined to torture himself with, and we had an insane attraction. All in all, there wasn't a whole lot more to it than that.

Especially since I hadn't really gotten a proper chance to show him who I was. Was I even his type? He'd only caught glimpses of me: a femme dude who could fuck rough. But there was so much more to me than just being femme, or being able to fuck hard. There were five hundred shades of fierceness in between, and he hadn't glimpsed any of it.

And I assumed that naturally, there was more to him, too. I saw him predominately through the filter of being my former bully—and unfortunately, I couldn't unsee or unhear his awful stand-up act—but that wasn't the whole picture, either. We might have known each other as small-town kids, but who were we now that we were fully realized adults?

I brought a ripe strawberry to my mouth and nibbled at it from the bottom. So, yeah, welcome to my life at the moment. If I wasn't consumed by work, I was ensnared in an incessant thoughtpool (like a whirlpool but, you know, made up of thoughts) of Miguel-inspired fantasies.

I grabbed my phone, my fingers eager to tap out a text to Miguel. We'd been in touch since I'd left. Every day, actually. But it was always low-key stuff, kinda hard to get deep and meaningful over text. He seemed interested in my work and loved hearing about how each show went, and while I tried to reciprocate and ask him about his day, I was discovering he was an expert deflector. His usual reply of "same day, different shit" would be followed by another text asking me about something.

I felt sad that Miguel's dream had crumbled that night. I was lucky. I got to do something for a living that didn't feel like work at all. It felt like a dream, one that took me all over the world, introduced me to a ton of interesting, creative people, and one that paid more in a year than my parents probably would ever earn in their lifetimes. Not that I didn't have to work my ass off to get my foot in the door—I got my toe in thanks to my uncle's friend's connection, but the first two years, gurrl, I paid my dues. But, yeah,

I was in a very good place when it came to my professional life. My personal life on the other hand...

I let out a long breath, pushed my entirely demolished dessert tray away, and rested my head against the headboard. What was going to happen with me and Miguel? I needed a sign...

And right on cue, my cell phone vibrated in my hand. It was a text. From Miguel.

Miguel: *Guess what?*
Me: *What?*
Miguel: *You have to guess.*
Me: *You have to give me more than that. Clue?*
Miguel: *Lemons into lemonade.*

Helpful. Not.

I paused, tapping my fingers on my chin until a flash of inspiration hit me.

Me: *New Beyoncé album?*
Miguel: *Hard no.*

Oh, okay...I had nothing else, my mind completely blank. Before I could scramble to text something—anything—back, my phone buzzed again.

Miguel: *I got an audition!!!*
Me: *Oh wow, that's great! Congratulations!*

But how on earth...?

Miguel: *Someone uploaded cell phone footage of my performance.*

That didn't make things *any* clearer. Luckily, Miguel seemed to have psychic texting abilities.

Miguel: *Long story short, the crew over at TMC (The Mean Comics) YouTube channel saw it, loved it, and they want me to audition for them.*
Me: *I'm really happy for you!*

I genuinely was.

That routine may have been terrible for the audience who had to suffer through it at Elysian, but mean comedy was a thing. If that's what he wanted to pursue, then he totally should. Not everyone liked classical music. It didn't mean there was anything wrong with it.

Life was about following *your* dreams, not anyone else's.

Me: *When's the audition?*
Miguel: *Next week.*
Me: *In LA? NYC?*
Miguel: *No.*
Miguel: *It's*
Miguel: *In*

Why was Miguel one-word texting?...

Miguel: *Philadelphia.*

Okay, that was why. My pulse ticked up a notch as my fingers tapped away furiously.

Me: *You should stay with me!*

I pressed *Send* before my brain could compute what I'd

written, and right after I did, a cold shiver skated up my spine. It was too much, too soon. There was no way Miguel would take me up on—

Miguel: *You sure?*

Shit. No. Maybe?

Grrr, why was this such a hard decision to make? I closed my eyes and inhaled. What did I want? What did I *really* want?

The answer came to me immediately. It was a no-brainer.

Me: *Of course. I've missed you.*

Shit version 2.0.

Someone please send out a search party for my brain. It fit perfectly into my head, was packed to the brim with all sorts of priceless insights into fashion and pop culture, and like the rest of me, was cute as fuck. Happy to pay a reward. No questions asked.

Miguel: *I've missed you too!*

Since we'd already assembled one search party for my brain, it wouldn't be too hard to tack on another one for my lungs, right, because how the fuck did a person breathe again?

I dropped the phone into my lap and slid down the headboard like a slug. A stupid, senseless, but oh so fucking happy, slug.

ONE WEEK LATER

24

MIGUEL

Emry offered to pick me up from the airport, but I refused. The guy was already letting me crash at his place. I didn't want to put him out any more.

I was a nervous wreck in the backseat of the Lyft, and it had nothing to do with my audition tomorrow and everything to do with Emry. I hadn't stopped thinking about him since he'd left Elysian three weeks ago, and even though this was a short in-and-out visit—hmm, yes, I went there, too—I'd take it. Heck, I'd do anything just to have some more time with him. Rainy rooftop sex an optional extra.

Sighing as a blur of lights, concrete, and shopfronts whizzed past my window, I wondered what it would be like. Now. Here. On his home turf.

I'd heard from plenty of guys who had gotten caught up in a romantic something-something under the warm breezes and sway of palm trees at Elysian, losing themselves in the uninhibited anything goes vibe of the place, but when they got home—and shit got real—the fun, light, vacation-love was gone. What'd been special and amazing in one environment didn't always translate to another place so well. Sometimes, a fling was just a fling.

Would this be the case with me and Emry? Not that we'd even gone so far as to have anything called a romantic something-something, but there was something more between us, more than just the physical connection. I was sure of it; I just didn't know whether we'd be able to pick up where we left off.

"Here you go," the driver announced as he pulled up in front of a restaurant, not an apartment building.

"Are you sure?" I checked my text message from Emry and read out the address as the driver said it aloud at the same time. Hmm, okay, so we were definitely at the right place. Maybe Emry lived above the restaurant? I looked up, but it was a single story building.

Slightly confused, I got out and started getting my luggage out of the trunk when a set of warm hands swaddled me and a hit of warm breath ignited the back of my neck. Spinning around, Emry's beaming face greeted me as my hands made their way around his waist.

"You made it." His voice was positively sparkling. "I've missed you."

"I missed you, too, Emry." I dropped my luggage and we embraced...until some asshole rudely interrupted our reunion because they had the audacity to want to pull into the empty car space we were kinda, sorta, totally hogging.

"Let me help you with that."

Before I could protest, Emry grabbed the smaller of the two bags and we vacated the space. He led me a few feet to the restaurant entrance. "I thought you might be hungry," he offered by way of explanation.

"I am." I slid my hand down the grooves of his stylish, navy blue quilted jacket.

The corner of his mouth curved. "For food."

"Oh, right. That."

We giggled all the way until we were seated in a corner table inside the dimly lit and tastefully decorated restaurant. We placed our orders, and another server came by to fill our glasses with water, and then it happened.

The first silence.

Yep. It was awkward, all right. I shifted my gaze, taking in the place, spending too much time studying the exposed brick walls and decor in all shades of brown, brass, and gold, like I was committing it to memory, while Emry fidgeted with the napkin, twirling it around his finger in one direction, unwrapping it and then twirling it in the other way.

Yeah. Screw Philly. Welcome to Awkwardsville.

"I really missed you, Emry." I repeated my earlier sentiment, hoping it would not only bridge the bumbling silence but let him know that even though I'd already said it once, I really meant it. Because I did. I'd missed him so much that it caught me by surprise at how intense the feelings were.

"Oh, yeah." Emry kept fumbling with the napkin, but his hazel eyes twinkled mischievously in the candlelight. "For how long? Until the next weekend when a new bunch of partygoers came to Elysian and you had your pick of new guests?"

He blinked the gleam away as he took in my reaction. I couldn't tell what my face was doing, but I felt a heaviness filling up my chest.

"I'm sorry, Miguel. That was a stupid joke. I didn't mean it." I looked up at him. His teeth were digging into his bottom lip. "I only said it because I'm super nervous and because..."

"Because what?" I asked tentatively after a beat.

"Because I haven't been able to stop thinking about you." His eyebrows squinched in tightly. "Why are you smiling?"

I reached across the table and placed my hand over his. "I haven't been able to stop thinking about you, either."

"But this will never work," he went on, as he slipped his hand out of mine, preferring the feel of napkin fabric than my touch. I should have been offended, but I wasn't.

"Never," I agreed wholeheartedly.

"This would be the worst idea ever."

"The worst."

"Like, so epically bad that there are no words."

"I should just get up right now, get my ass back to Florida, and we should never see each other again."

Our eyes locked. My breath hitched in my throat, and Emry's teeth resumed assaulting his lower lip.

"Or..." Emry's fingers found mine again (take that, stupid napkin; I was only pretending not to be jealous of you), "we could enjoy the time we do have together. The food here is amazing."

"Uh-huh."

God, his fingers were so silky smooth. I remembered thinking that the first time we touched. I guess I expected them to be hardened from all his piano playing, but nope, they were as soft and silky smooth as I'd remembered.

"And the desserts here are to die for." Emry practically swooned. "Tonight, I was thinking we might want to go with—"

"You."

Emry's mouth parted slightly and my cock stirred. It was a preview of the direction I was about to take this conversation in.

"For dessert, Emry, I'd like something that's not on the menu: *you*."

He sucked in his lip, and hesitation mixed with something else crossed his face. "You don't know me, Miguel. I mean, not really. And the same is true of me. I don't really know you that well, either."

"I believe," I leaned in, "that's the whole point of doing this talking thing, right? Besides, we do know each other. We have a history."

"But we're different now, too." Emry's voice took on a weighty tone. "I'm not the same person I was back then, and, Miguel, neither are you."

His words struck me right in the center of my chest.

I'd spent so many years punishing myself, drowning in guilt from the shitty behavior of my past, that in some ways, I was still wrapped up in being that person, that version of myself. Sure, I'd grown, I'd matured, but I never allowed myself to forget what I had done to him.

Hearing Emry acknowledge that we were both different felt like...actually, I didn't know what it felt like. Good? Freeing? Underpinned by a burning question of *did I deserve it*?

Was it possible for us to start over? Was that what he wanted? Did that mean there was a possibility that out of the smoldering embers of our past, we could create an *us* in our future?

While I was busy freefalling into my own deep pit of insecurity, I hadn't even noticed that Emry was doing pretty much the exact same thing. It wasn't until his words jarred me back to reality that I got an insight into how he was dealing with all of this.

A darkness tinted his eyes. "Dating hasn't been easy for me."

I cleared my throat to calm my nerves a bit. "Can I ask why?"

"It's hard to date when you're...feminine acting, looking, talking, sounding like me. Most gay dudes hate it."

"I don't."

He squinted at me, and I could sense the suspicion behind the look. "I like that you're femme, Emry. I've always liked that about you."

His squint deepened. His eyes were basically slits at this point. "Why?"

It was a fair question and I totally deserved for him not to believe me. I didn't want to spin up some bullshit answer, so I went with what was in my heart. "I admire the way you are because it's real. It's true. You're not pretending to be somebody else."

He remained frozen, the only movement being an occasional blink. Okay, I had to go deeper. "When I look at you, Emry, I don't see the flailing hand actions or the outrageous clothes—although you do have exquisite fashion taste—or the campy expressions. No. I see something else."

His breath trembled. "What?"

"I see *you*, Emry. You're not hiding behind any of that stuff, but I also know that it's only a part of you. A big part, sure. A fabulous part. But it's, like, only a preview, not the main attraction. And I like what I see."

Emry let out a tiny smile and with flushed cheeks, pressed on. "You've only seen one side of me, Miguel."

"Give me a chance to see more, Emry. Please. I don't know how I know this, but I have a feeling that the more you show me, the more I'll like you. And believe me, I like you a lot already. Let me really, *really* like you."

25

EMRY

Did Miguel really just say that?

And was my mind suddenly inundated with memes of Sally Field's "You really like me" Oscars acceptance speech? That would be a yes, on both fronts. I pushed Sally aside (sorry, gurl) and focused on the earnest dreamboat sitting in front of me.

Let's get one thing straight—I didn't need anyone's permission or approval. I lived my life for me, and fuck everyone else. But damn, it felt so good hearing him say those words. I reminded myself that they were just words, but they were on the same frequency as his apology: genuine. I felt it deep in my bones, and I could tell he meant them.

The server returned to our table. "Some wine?"

Miguel gave a shrug, so I said, "Yes. Thank you."

I needed some help processing how this evening had gone so far. Seeing Miguel stepping out of the car reignited the fire that hadn't really been stamped out since we'd last seen each other. He hadn't spotted me as he went to get his luggage from the trunk, but there was no way I could've missed him. He was dressed smartly, and god, that plain black T-shirt molded to his body like it'd been painted on.

I stepped in behind him, inhaling his familiar sweet scent, and let out a relieved sigh. It felt as good to see him as I'd remembered. Better, even.

And the way dinner was going, I'd be seeing a whole lot more of him later, too. Miguel finished off his meal, while I sipped on the wine. He told me a little more about the audition he had tomorrow, but my hearing was clearly selective. When he said it was at eleven, all I could think about was that it meant we could sleep in together...after a long night of—

"Emry, hello?"

Miguel waved a hand in front of me. "Were you even listening to me?"

"Uh, of course I was." I gulped down some more wine.

His eyes were as wide as his smile. "Great, then you won't mind answering my question."

Crap on a stick! Question, hey. Assuming it was of the yes/no variety, I had a fifty-fifty chance of getting it right, so I went with what I hoped sounded like an assured, "Yes."

He broke into chuckles behind his hand.

"What?" I said, trying to keep my cool and not sound too exasperated.

"I didn't ask you a question."

"Oh." I could feel my blush rising up my neck. "If it makes a difference, I was thinking about you."

"Then you're instantly forgiven," Miguel said with another light chuckle. He placed his palms flat on the table, swerving his head from side to side as he moved in. "Was it something dirty?"

Now it was my turn to giggle. I nodded. "Filthy, actually."

He licked that full lower lip of his teasingly, like he knew exactly the effect it had on me. "Tell me more."

I glanced around. No one was in earshot, so I figured why not? I tapped my fingers on the table, summoning the perfect words. And then they came. Divine inspiration. It was based on what Miguel had said before we'd had sex in Florida that had stuck with me all this time. The bit where he looked over his shoulder and instructed me to fuck him like I hated him. Except now, I had my own twist to add to it. One that I hoped he liked.

I lowered my head and he matched my movement. "Miguel." I paused, drawing out the anticipation of the moment for as long as possible. His tongue dangled adorably out the side of his mouth, his dark eyes glimmering with desire.

"Tonight, I don't want to fuck you like I hate you. I want to fuck you like...I like you."

26

MIGUEL

The walk back to Emry's place was short since he only lived two blocks away. Or maybe it was long, took two hours, and we were carried by a fleet of flying unicorns through a rainbow-filled sky. I had no fucking idea because my brain went completely haywire after Emry uttered those words to me at the restaurant.

He wanted to fuck me like *he liked me*. Was that what he'd actually said?

Good thing then that all I needed for sex was lips, hands, and a rock-hard cock.

His apartment was nice. Had walls, doors and, uh, what's the word for those thingies? Oh yeah, furniture. It was kinda hard to see any of it, though. At some point, I'd scooped Emry into my arms, and now I found myself walking backward down a darkened hallway with Emry writhing around in my arms.

Oomph.

My back hit a wall. Emry pulled his face off mine, his eyes wide, but all I saw was those puffy, just-kissed lips. "Are you okay?"

"No." I replied solemnly, stilling myself against the wall. "You've stopped kissing me."

His lips pulled upward. "I can remedy that. We're almost there. My room is the last one." I followed his eyes, before slamming my mouth into his and resuming down the corridor.

Emry kicked open his bedroom door and we stumbled into the room. I flung both of us onto his bed and before we'd stopped bouncing from the impact, I was already tearing at his clothes. He looked so pretty in them, but he'd look a thousand times better with them on the floor.

"I meant what I said," Emry whispered into my mouth. "I want this time to be different."

"What if I like it rough?" My fingers smoothed over his jawline, dropping down into the hollows of his neck.

"Do you?"

I swallowed hard. I had no intention of lying to him. "I do, Emry. I like being...manhandled."

A smile spread slowly across his face. "Rough but soft. I can do that."

My cock leaked at those words. How was it possible that Emry was giving me everything I had ever wanted?

With clothes off, I wriggled up the bed, grabbing lube and condoms from the side table. Handing them to him, I offered, "If we're going soft, then no prep. The first thing I want to feel inside me is your cock."

His cheeks heated and I rolled over onto my stomach. After a few seconds, Emry's arms landed on either side of my body, something hard and wet pressing against my ass. He softly threaded his fingers through my hair before digging in sharply. The contrast ignited me and sharpened all my senses, tuning them to him with an exact precision.

His chest fell onto my back, the pressure pinning me against the mattress. It felt divine. He kissed the back of my neck and across my shoulders. I turned and lifted my head, our warm lips locking. He let out a delicate moan, the sound skittering across my skin.

"Claim me," I whisper-ordered into his mouth. "Make me yours."

A heat flared in his eyes and he lifted his chest off me. His cock, which had been teasing my hole, entered me. I hissed, the screeching jolt of tension around my ass setting me on fire. "More," I demanded.

And that's exactly what he gave me, thrusting deep into me until I felt his balls slap the backs of my thighs. His fingers found my hair again, and as he settled into a steady rhythm, he controlled not only my entire body, but my head as well, tugging me with a wild abandon.

"You're so beautiful, Miguel."

I loved giving myself over like this. He had total control over me and it was the most blissful feeling in the universe. His pace picked up as his fingernails scratched into my scalp. The burning sensation collided with the fullness of him in me. I was lying flat on my stomach, so I had no way of reaching my cock which was pinned under me, but I had a feeling I wasn't going to have to touch it with my hands.

The friction between my rock-hard dick and the mattress felt incredible as Emry nailed me harder and harder. "So good." The words escaped me as my body rocked under Emry's exquisite control.

"Getting close," he huffed.

"Wait," I said suddenly. "Flip me over. I want to look into your eyes when you come."

Emry stopped what felt like mid-thrust. I was expecting him to pull out and roll me over. I didn't think there was any other way of doing it. Turns out, I was sooo wrong.

With his cock still halfway inside me, he pushed my knees up the bed and reached under my shoulders. No way. Surely he wasn't going to—

With a gentle but strong twist, he started to turn me over, while he was still inside me. The sensation was incredible. The changing angle meant he was hitting spots inside of me I didn't know existed. Carefully, he laid me down on my back, pushed in until he was as far inside of me as he could be, and hovered over me.

I flicked a loose strand of hair from his face. "That was..."

Emry smiled knowingly as he began thrusting his hips. "Oh god, this is..."

Shit. Why was I unable to finish a sentence?

Oh, that's right. Because Emry was giving me the best, strongest yet tender fuck of my life.

"You okay?" Emry asked.

I groaned against his deepening thrusts. "Yeah. Amazing. So good." At least, that's what I think came out of my mouth. I couldn't be sure, but I did know one thing. Being able to see Emry's face was the best thing in the world.

He kicked up his rhythm to *oh my fucking Lord* levels, and

before I knew what was happening, my head was spinning, bright gold dots appeared in my line of sight, and my entire chest up to my chin was smeared with a warm coating of cum.

"Wait, did you come, too?" I asked, still in a dizzying trance.

Emry pulled out of me and giggled. "Uh, yeah." He pulled the condom off his cock and showed me the evidence. "Like a fucking fountain."

He got up and disappeared to what I assumed was his en suite bathroom. When he returned, he held a warm washcloth in his hand. "May I?"

My brain was still offline, but I nodded anyway, even though I was unsure what I was agreeing to.

With the most tender care I had ever experienced, Emry began to wipe down my stomach, chest, and jaw. I'd never had someone clean me up before and the sweetness of it was almost too much for my heart to handle.

I grabbed his forearm, mid-stroke. He looked at me quizzically. "You okay, Miguel?"

I shook my head. "Can you—can you hold me? Please."

A soft look fell across his features as Emry wordlessly threw the washcloth onto the floor. A few breaths later, I was snuggled up in his warm embrace. His heart thumped against my back, its steady beat providing me much needed reassurance.

As I nestled even closer, removing any gaps between our skin, I closed my eyes and let out a breath as my newest realization settled over me.

Soft sex was the most amazing thing in the world.

27
EMRY

The next morning, I tiptoed as quietly as I could out of my bedroom and down the hallway, but I could have just as easily been floating on air because O...to the M...to the G. Last night felt like the most decadent dream, and if I wasn't able to still taste Miguel's sweetness on my lips, I might have thought that's what it was.

A lost and wayward part of me had found its way home somewhere between my last glass of wine at the restaurant and the moment Miguel had asked me to spin him around so that we could look into each other's faces as we came.

What we'd done last night wasn't just sex, and it wasn't lovemaking either. It was a healing, a monumental shift in the way we saw each other. And my god, it was so, *so* tender. The memory of it was making my heart ache. I needed to experience that again in my life.

I slipped into my kitchen. Making as little noise as possible, I set about making Miguel a delicious breakfast comprised of the two main morning food groups: pancakes and syrup. I was so lost in my own little world that I hadn't noticed Miguel's footsteps as he padded into the kitchen. I startled as I felt a warm hand graze my shoulder.

"Sorry." He sounded sleepy. "Didn't mean to scare you."

I spun around. With his hair clumped to his forehead and his groggy eyes struggling to remain open, his appearance caused a stirring in my stomach. "Sleep well?" I asked, swiping my fingers through his hair.

"Like a baby. What's all this?"

"I am making you breakfast," I declared proudly as I twisted back around. "We worked up quite an appetite last night."

"Mmm, we sure did." He thrust his hardening cock against my thigh. "But I could always go another round."

"No time, mister," I shot back. Miguel nestled his chin into the nook of my shoulder. "We slept in. It's almost ten. Your audition's in just over an hour."

He stepped away, but before I could turn to see where he'd

gone, he propped himself up onto the countertop, dipping his finger into the batter.

"Shoo." I smiled, patting his hand away.

He caught my fingers in his. "Are you okay with everything that happened last night?"

I stopped what I was doing and looked straight into those two dark pools. "I am, Miguel. What about you?"

He dipped his chin to his chest before returning my gaze. A fire ignited behind his irises. "You have no idea, Emry. As my right hand can attest, I've been wanting that all my life. I just—I just..."

He lowered his head as the words trailed away.

"Just what, Miguel?" I hooked the side of my index finger under his chin, lifting his face to mine. "It's okay. You can tell me. I won't judge you. I would never judge you based on anything we do in there." I tipped my head toward the bedroom.

He nodded gratefully. "I know you wouldn't. And that's what I mean, Emry. I just never thought that I could have it all with someone."

I caressed his cheek. "What do you mean?"

"Well, in my experience, sex didn't match up with the way I felt for a guy. I like a certain kind of sex, and I never thought that I'd find someone who I actually really liked who was compatible with me in that regard. It was always sex over here"—he pointed to his left—"and feelings over here." He pointed to his right. "But with you, I have everything I've ever wanted right here." He clutched at his heart, and how I was still able to stay standing on my two feet, I had no idea.

I reached out, grabbed his hand from his chest, and cupped it over my heart. "I'm here to tell ya, that sex and those feelings you have live right here for me, too."

A lightness flashed over his handsome features before he broke out into a massive smile. "Thank you, Emry. You have no idea how much that means."

He was wrong. I did. But I didn't say anything. I knew more

than a thing or two about not being able to be my true self when it came to sex, scared that people would judge me or assume certain things. While there were a lot of things that were different about our experience, there was a lot that was the same.

"I'm almost done here." I pointed toward the stove top. "Why don't you jump in the shower?"

With a sprightly nod, he pushed himself off the counter, brushing his lips against my cheek as he left. I twirled around after him as he trundled down the hallway, and yes, I may have totally checked out his tight little bubble butt.

As I got breakfast ready, I noticed something. For the first time in a very long time, I was feeling things. More astonishing, I was doing something completely and totally unlike me—I was actually letting myself feel them. I caught my reflection in the microwave and holy shit, I was smiling. Feeling and smiling, both at the same time. I raced to the window. Nope, the sky hadn't fallen in. Fancy that.

I couldn't pinpoint the moment it happened. Maybe it wasn't one standalone moment but the combination of a series of smaller ones, but Miguel had managed to unlock a deeply held, tucked away part of me. The crazy thing was...it wasn't the worst thing in the world. In fact, it all felt good. So damn good.

"Whatcha thinkin' about?"

Miguel returned wearing one of my totally nerdy *only around the house* sweaters. It was gray. Let me rephrase that: it was *just* gray. No way I'd ever let anyone ever see me in something so...plain.

"I hope you don't mind," he said sheepishly, tugging at his top, "but I saw it in the bathroom and couldn't resist. It smells like you."

I blushed. "It's fine," I replied, making my way past him and to the table. It was a little tight on him, but I didn't mind the way it accentuated his wide shoulders and massive arms.

"Breakfast is served," I managed to say while successfully avoiding direct eye contact. This all felt good, too good, so of course, the first crack in my thoughts had to emerge, didn't it? Good was good, but how long could it possibly last for?

We started eating in silence. I wasn't paying attention to the pancakes. I was too busy mulling things over in my head. Did I dare do it? Allow myself to fall for him, slip into something that I've wanted for so long but hadn't prioritized in my life? An actual romantic relationship.

"We should talk," we both said at the same time.

"You first," I said with a friendly wave.

"No, no, you go first," Miguel insisted.

I put my fork down and interlaced my fingers. Since I couldn't find anything to say about what I was feeling, I decided to open with a question. "What's happening here, Miguel?"

"So, you feel it, too?"

I nodded and probably grinned like an idiot as well at his inadvertent admission. I wasn't the only one feeling what was unfolding here between us. Fuck a Destiny's Child reunion. My number one prayer looked like it was being answered.

"The truth is, I like you, Emry. A lot. And while I can think of plenty of reasons why this is insane and probably won't work out— and believe me, I've been driving myself crazy thinking about pretty much nothing else—I keep circling back to those three little words, 'I like you.'"

"I like you, too," I added with a smile. "And I want to get to know you better."

"Same."

I glanced down at my watch and blew out a noisy breath. The realization dawned on me. This was our first and only chance to talk. Miguel was jumping on a flight right after his audition, and we didn't have the time we needed to talk this through properly.

Dammit. Why did Florida have to be so far away?

"We need to talk more," I said.

"Yes. We do."

"But we don't have the time right now."

Miguel smiled but it didn't reach anywhere near his eyes. "So, what should we do?"

A heavy lump lodged in my throat. "We'll be in touch. We'll figure something out." I couldn't tell which one of us I was trying to convince. "But you need to get your head into the game. You've got an audition to get ready for and Miguel, you are going to kill it."

28

MIGUEL

There's a glaring double standard in the comedy world and it hit me in the face the second I walked into the reception area at The Mean Comic's head office. Female comedians might not always have been what is considered conventionally attractive, but they at least put in some effort. Here, I felt like I'd stumbled into schlep central as I was greeted by a bunch of unshaven, sloppily dressed, and possibly unshowered guys, if the smell in the room was anything to go by.

I sat down next to a guy whose *Big Dick Energy* T-shirt didn't quite cover his beer belly. Don't get me wrong. There was no fat shaming here. I was a chubby kid myself and would never make fun of someone's size. But the guy had a glazed look in his eyes (I was thinking stoned, maybe?) and looked a lot like the human equivalent of serial drunk Barney from *The Simpsons*. I half expected him to greet me with a belch. Instead, I got a disgruntled-sounding, "Hey" from him.

I smiled and said, "Hey" back as I sat down beside him. Thankfully, he wasn't in the mood to expand on the sparkling start of our conversation, and I was glad for the silence, too. It gave me a chance to process the events of last night...and the conversation we'd had over breakfast this morning.

I always thought I'd have to separate my life because the various bits and pieces that made up who I was didn't always gel neatly together. I liked sex rough, with a sprinkling of submission. In my mind, that didn't exactly sit well with being the kinda guy you'd bring home to meet your parents. I'd resigned myself to the fact that the type of sex I liked would be restricted to anonymous hookups with guys I could be uninhibited with, and a relationship would mean settling down and vanilla-izing myself to fit into the mold of a "good boyfriend."

That separation filtered into non-sex areas of my life as well, such as my fledgling comedic career. As much as I enjoyed clean comedy, part of me gravitated toward mean comedy and filthy jokes where no topic was off-limits and no one was safe. But offstage? I wasn't an asshole. I did my best to do my best. Yet how could one person be both? Weren't you meant to choose one path over the other? Wasn't that how it worked?

That's what I always thought, and I guess that's why I had subconsciously delayed making a real start in pursuing my comedy dreams for as long as possible. It felt like a hard choice to make, one I wasn't ready for just yet.

And then last night happened, and it dawned on me—somewhere between Emry thrusting slowly into me and whispering how beautiful I was, right before I came so hard I almost blacked out—that maybe, just maybe, I didn't have to choose.

Perhaps having it all was an option?

The conversation between the two guys sitting to my left yanked me out of my hope-filled—and let's face it, probably as likely as a Kardashian winning the Nobel Peace Prize—future, as their words drifted over to me.

"I hear they're developing their first ever scripted show," the guy closest to me said.

"No way," the other guy responded, sounding personally offended. "That would be a total sell-out. Stand-up is true comedy. Everything else is bullshit."

I frowned. I wouldn't necessarily agree with that. A lot of my favorite comedians started off as stand-ups, but it was only once they landed a network show that they reached a larger audience and achieved fame. I didn't care about the fame part. I was happy being more of a behind-the-scenes guy. But being able to reach millions of people and make them laugh? Now *that* got my creative juices flowing.

Seeing as this was my first ever audition, I had no idea what to expect when my name was called by a perky-sounding twelve-year-old kid whose clipboard was almost as wide as his shoulders. I followed him down an obscenely white-walled corridor.

We stepped into a large room that looked like a mini-version of what you'd see at a comedy club. There was a stage with the requisite brown wall backdrop, a mic stand, one big lighting rig shining a spotlight onto the mic, and four directors' chairs in the audience section. Sitting in them were three guys and one fiercely ginger-haired woman with ridiculous oversized, black-rimmed glasses and her hair messily tied up in a bun at the top of her head.

I was so nervous I didn't quite catch their names. "So, we saw your video," the guy next to the woman drawled in a total uninterested hipster way. "We were really impressed." His words, like, sooo didn't match his tone.

"That's great, thank you so much," I gushed way too enthusiastically. I auto-corrected to save face. "I mean, yeah, whatever." Was that better? Worse? Dammit, I was sweating bullets and the audition hadn't even started yet.

After some more awkward to and fro-ing, I finally got up onto the stage. As soon as my fingers laced around the mic, the tension in my chest eased. I had prepared some new material, edgier than what I'd performed at Elysian. Yes, that *was* possible to do. While I had misjudged the crowd there, I knew that with these guys, the dirtier the better.

I'll spare the details, but my act drew out an impressive number of gasps from the panel, as well as giggles and laughs in all the right places, too. No topic was off-limits and no one had been spared, especially not that poor ferret that was the punchline in my Trump bit.

For me, performing it was a mixed bag. While I felt fine doing it, that was all I felt: just fine. It wasn't lighting up my insides like I expected it might. I'd been nervous beforehand, but during the set, I was totally calm and remained focused with a Zen-like precision. The overall effect meant that as I wrapped up my time with them and was being escorted out of the room by the preteen, the main feeling I was left with was a sort of numbness.

This should have been exhilarating, my first real and big proper step in reaching a lifelong dream to pursue a career in comedy. But if this was what I'd been wanting my whole life, why was I so blasé about the whole thing? It shouldn't have felt like a gargantuan effort to muster up even the slightest bit of enthusiasm about it.

As I left the building and jumped into a taxi headed to the airport, I could tell that something was off. Now if only I had the faintest inkling as to what that could possibly be.

THREE DAYS LATER

29

EMRY

"He stayed with you?"

With the way Hawk's jaw had bunched up and the daggers that were flying out of his eyes, you'd think I'd invited Jared and Ivanka to join us on our next trip to Elysian.

"He did," I replied, casually perusing the brunch menu as we sat outside at a cute new cafeteria that had recently opened on 13th Street in Midtown Village. "Miguel was only in town for one night, had the audition the next day, and then went straight back to Florida."

My heart tugged at the heaviness of the words. It had only been three days since he had left, but man, I missed him. A lot.

"Did you fuck?"

"Geez, Hawk. Letta girl have a mimosa before you bring out the F word."

We were in the part of Philly that was officially known as The Gayborhood, so I wasn't worried about anyone overhearing our conversation and judging us. Hawk's bullish demeanor, though? Yeah, that was strange. It meant that the time had finally come for us to properly talk about Miguel. Hawk's protectiveness of me, which I appreciated, was based on an incomplete picture of the guy, and it was time to fill in some of the blanks.

After the server took our orders, I faced him and said, "I think we should talk about Miguel."

Hawk's shoulders stiffened. "Uh-huh." He picked up the menu and studied it, even though we'd just finished placing our orders.

I gently lifted the menu away from him. "Hawk."

I waited for him to look at me. It took a while, but eventually, we got there. "You're one of my best friends, and I can't tell you how much it means to me that you care about me and want what's best for me."

His eyes softened. "I really do, Emry. You're such a special person. You'll never be with someone as good as you, but whatever guy you're with needs to be a close second."

I smiled, basking for a moment in his lovely sentiment. "Thank you." I paused for a moment before going on. "I know you have reservations about Miguel."

"That obvious, huh?" Hawk scratched behind his neck.

"Uh, yeah. Even the crew up in the International Space Station called it."

Hawk let out a chuckle and the deep rumble of it eased my tension. We were such good friends. I knew we'd be able to work this out.

"I can see why there are a couple of reasons for you to not like Miguel."

"His comedy. The fact that he bullied you in high school," Hawk pointed out, lifting his fingers as he listed each point.

"Yes. Exactly. It's all out in the open. Both of those things are true, Hawk. But so is this." I looked him straight in the eye as I said it. "I like him, and he likes me."

My words clouded Hawk's eyes, and his expression shifted to something I couldn't get a proper read on.

I continued. "There is stuff that we have to work through obviously, and we are. But I need you to know that something is happening between us, and I'd really like it if you trusted me and supported me as I figure this out. Hawk, I need you. You're one of my best friends."

I would have thought that little reminder would have earned me a smile. Instead, his lips were doing something that looked a whole lot like scowling.

After a longer than usual silence, he gave a clipped nod. "Sure. Of course. I'm here for you, man. As your friend."

Something about the way he spat out the word *friend* at the end left a bitterness simmering in the air between us. Thankfully, it was soon replaced by smells of bacon, eggs, and pancakes as our breakfasts arrived.

"So, what's been happening with you?" I asked, taking a bite and hoping a change in topic might be in order.

Talking was never really Hawk's strong point, but with the

right combination of gentle prodding and not insisting on filling every single silent patch with words, he usually opened up. As he dug into his breakfast, he filled me in on some renovations he was doing at his house, how he'd been killing it at the gym and bench pressed three hundred pounds (I smiled politely as if I had any clue what those words in that sequence actually meant), and then he resorted to his usual grumblings about how unfair it was that there were only twenty-four hours in a day when he was trying to get his side hustle plumbing business off the ground.

But after all of that, his focus returned back to me with an even greater sharpness than before. "Well?" His thick fingers tapped the edge of the table. "Did you fuck him?" This time, his bark was subsumed by something softer, sadder.

I finished chewing and wiped the corners of my mouth. "Yeah, I did."

It felt a little weird to be talking to Hawk about sex—and maybe that's what he was picking up on, too?—since for the better part of the last few years, Hawk was a witness to it. At least, for me. I'm sure he was getting plenty of action on his own, although funnily enough, he never really talked about it.

As sad as it sounded, my only sex action over the past few years was limited to the crazy adventures Hawk and I got up to at Elysian. After a self-imposed ban from hookup apps and with my crazy touring schedule, meeting guys for sex by myself hadn't been a priority. Until recently—until Miguel—the idea of sex without Hawk felt almost unimaginable.

"This is a bit weird, isn't it?" I asked, trying to lighten the mood a bit.

Hawk's cheeks went rosy. "What do you mean?"

"Well, normally, we don't talk about sex since we're both, you know, there for it. Together."

His blush only reddened. "Uh, yeah. That's it."

We sank into another silence as we ate. Okay, so I was a little out of practice having post-sex chats with my bestie, but at the same time, I didn't feel like sharing the details of my time with Miguel. It felt too special and too private to share over brunch, even with Hawk.

And the more my thoughts swirled about Miguel, I couldn't help but grin as I ate.

"What are you smiling at?"

I shrugged, trying to play it off. It'd make the weirdness between Hawk and me even more pronounced, but it hit me clear as day—I was falling deeper and deeper for Miguel Cortez.

TEN DAYS LATER

30
_____

MIGUEL

I missed him.

I knew it was dumb and it made no logical sense, but I did. It got me so stupid and affected that I was pacing up and down my tiny apartment, even though my feet were killing me after working my ninth day in a row. We'd been short-staffed at the resort, and even though it meant overriding Leo's objections, I filled in. The team needed me and I wasn't going to let them down.

But the really ludicrous thing that I'd done? That would've been the text I'd just pressed *Send* on.

To Emry.

Telling him I missed him.

Shit. I may have had close to zero experience when it came to the whole dating scene—including calling it a scene to begin with— but I was pretty sure you had to play it a little cool. And sending an *I miss you* text might have been a lot of things, but cool wasn't one of them.

I stared down at my cell phone. I'd been clutching it with a white-knuckled tightness for all one hundred and twenty seconds since sending the message, and yes, it had officially been the longest two minutes in the history of humanity. In all of that time, I think I'd taken a grand total of four breaths. It's kinda hard to breathe when your heart is beating outta your throat.

What the hell was I thinking? As if Emry would be interested in a guy like me. I was his former bully who—because he's such a wonderful guy—he'd taken pity on. Okay, throw a little life-altering sex into the mix, but that could just be him getting some revenge. No, wait. That was definitely the wrong word.

I hummed, tapping my fingers on my chin. Closure, perhaps. That was better. He got to fuck his former bully like a little bitch and ta-da(!), full circle moment. He could now move on with his life, while I wallowed in anguish and spiraled into an ever increasingly nonsensical delirium, but could you really blame me for panicking? I was approaching the three minute mark and still, no response from Emry.

My mini freak-out was kinda illogical since Emry had told me that he liked me when I visited him in Philly before my audition. But that was almost two weeks ago now. The more time passed, the more I began to get worried that what we'd had was slipping away from us before it got the chance to get a proper start. His exact words were fading in my memory and I was afraid that's where all of this was heading: into Memorysville.

We'd been texting every day, and while that was nice, what we actually needed to do was have a conversation. A proper one. Ideally, it would be great if we could do it while being in the same state. But Emry was in New York, performing another short concert run, and my life was here in Florida.

This thing between us was never going to happen. We may have had feelings and an attraction to each other, but the practicality of our reality conspired cruelly against us.

I glared at my phone, willing it to yield to my silent demands of a response. I threw it onto the couch in disgust. Why hadn't he texted me ba—

My phone buzzed and I lunged at it like I was a hero in an action movie jumping to hit the control panel to stop the bomb that would destroy the world from detonating. Fanciful? Totally. As if I'd ever be the good guy.

I lined the text up on my screen, but before facing it, I took a deep breath to calm myself down. When that did nothing except for getting me even more anxious, I decided to fuck serenity and just read the damn text.

Emry: *I miss you too.*

Oh, thank fuck.

I flopped over the back of the couch and hugged the phone into my chest, cradling it as if it were a baby. With my feet dangling in the air, I texted back immediately. Because text efficiency was a totally cool smooth move that guys responded well to, right?

Me: *I want to see you. When does your run in NYC end?*
Emry: *That would be nice. I'd like to see you too! Our last show is next Thursday.*
Me: *Don't suppose you'd like to fly down to Elysian that weekend?*

I stayed frozen on the couch, with my legs dangling in the air, unable to move into a more comfortable position, preferably one that didn't involve the flow of blood going straight to my head.

Was it possible to age in less than thirty seconds? I flicked to the camera app on my phone and scoured my hair for the first signs of any gray hairs. The waiting was killing me. Was he toying with me? Was he enjoying subjecting me to this torture?

Emry: *Hmm...I could be convinced.*
Me: *Is that your not so subtle way of asking me for a dick pic? Because if it gets you down here, I'll Google how to take one and send it to you.*
Emry: *LOL. No. Um, and seriously, you've never sent a dick pic?*
Me: *I swear. Never.*
Emry: *I don't know why, but for some reason, I like that. For the record, I haven't either.*
Me: *That's just wrong. Your dick is magnificent. It's so fine it should have its own YouTube channel.*
Emry: *I'm pretty sure that would violate all of their terms and conditions, so I'm going to change subjects now... I don't want a dick pic, but I won't object to a face pic. You know, to help me make up my mind about whether I should come down and visit.*

Fuck. I took the worst selfies ever. I had no idea about angles, lighting, or any of that other life-essential stuff. My face only seemed to have two expressions that showed up in photos: a slightly exasperated one that looked like I was about to let one rip, or a self-satisfied smug that looked like I *had* let one rip.

Neither option was the cool or smooth maneuver I was hoping for here.

Me: *Tell you what...how about we take a selfie—together—when you come down here?*

I rapped my fingers along my thigh, expecting another torturous multi-minute wait when my phone vibrated again. Before I read the message, I squeezed my eyes shut and actually said out loud, "Please make him say yes."

Emry: *Deal!*
Emry: *And maybe throw in a hole pic for my private collection?*

I smiled goofily.

Miguel: *Done and done.*
Emry: *Cool. I'll book the flight tonight.*
Miguel: *Can't wait to see you!!!*
Emry: *Same here!!!*

ELEVEN DAYS LATER

31

EMRY

It was a last-minute trip, but not only could Hawk make it, he made it sound like it was no bother to clear what I thought was his jam-packed schedule. So much for whining about the lack of hours in the day. He also didn't grumble about the fact that we had to catch the last flight out of Philly on a Friday night, which meant that we wouldn't get in a day earlier like we normally did. Our usual suite was also booked out, but again, not a single complaint from the guy. Although secretly, I kinda hoped I wouldn't be spending a whole lot of time in the room, anyway.

I didn't mind that Hawk was tagging along. We always had a good time together, although I would have to advise him that our dick twin arrangement had to be put on ice, at least for a little while. Even if a small part of me hoped that *for a little while* actually translated to a long while.

It was a beautiful clear Saturday morning as I strutted alongside the edge of the resort's magnificent centerpiece pool. I could practically hear people's necks snapping in my direction, taking me in. All of me. I was feeling my oats and living for the fierce look I was rocking. From head to toe, I was truly a sight to behold.

My body was hugged in the most beautiful, light and gloriously pink kaftan I had sewn together from three different shades of pink material and bedazzled the fuck out of. And my feet? They were on fleek in a pair of glittery wedge flip-flops. I seriously had a come to Jesus moment the second I spied them in the shop front window display—I almost fainted when the attendant told me they had one last pair available...and in my size!

But my fierce *lewk* wasn't about impressing the guests at the resort who were making their way to the pool area for a day of lounging and relaxing. No, I wanted to make a grand entrance for a mini-reunion. A very special reunion.

I reached four deckchairs in prime poolside position, flailed my arms to showcase the wondrous creation I was wearing, and declared my arrival with a loud and campy as fuck pronouncement. "Extra, extra, kaftan all about it!"

"Holy fucking shitballs," Cassius cried out as he shot up from his deckchair and embraced me in the bear hug to end all bear hugs. "How are you, man?"

When he loosened his grip and I was able to resume normal breathing, I took in my friend. We'd met at the resort almost a year ago. Instant connection. When you meet someone and you just know you're gonna be friends? Yep, that was him and me.

"I didn't come here to play," I declared, looping my arms around his neck. "I came here to slay!"

After a round of giggles, I shimmied past Cass to his super-duper, cute as a peach boyfriend, Spencer. They'd been friends since the first day of first grade but had gotten together here at Elysian. Hawk and I had front row seats to seeing their relationship transform, especially since up until they came to Elysian, Spencer had identified as straight. It was so special to be a witness to something so heartwarming and beautiful. It was just as nice watching it unfold over the last year, through texts, calls, and emails with them both.

"Guuurl, we have *a lot* to catch up on."

"We sure do," Cassius agreed enthusiastically.

Hawk and Spencer kindly offered to get us drinks. It was only a little after ten, so we went with a sensible early-morning option: a margarita pitcher and beers. *Light* beers. Cass also placed an order for a burger with two sides of fries because, as he informed the group, breakfast had been well over an hour ago.

"So," he leaned in and grabbed my forearm, "I heard someone's fallen for a stand-up comedian."

I readjusted my Gucci glasses. "Hawk spilled?"

"Gushed like a waterfall. I've never heard the guy say so many words. Didn't think he was capable of it, frankly."

We giggled before I turned to Cassius and dove straight into the heart of it. "I'm really into him, Cass. I don't know if Hawk told you, but Miguel and I have a history together, but...but I also really want us to have a future, too."

Sensing the seriousness that had washed over me, Cassius' green eyes narrowed. "Emry, I am here for you. I am your sounding board, wingman, and if required, food taste tester. Use me as needed. Because like you reminded me a few times when Spencer and I came down here, you have to follow your heart."

"Did I really say that?"

"Well, either you or Hallmark movies, but I got it from somewhere."

We were still laughing when the guys returned with our drinks and Cassius' burger.

"Cheers," Spencer toasted, lifting his glass. We cheersed and before I'd had a chance to take a proper sip, Spencer lobbed a question straight at me. "So, you're here to see your new boyfriend?"

I met his sing-song taunt with an equally mature eye roll and groan. "He's not my boyfriend." Then, as I shuffled back into the deckchair, I added cheekily, "Not yet, anyway."

That drew some excited "Oohs" from Cass and Spencer. Hawk, on the other hand, was lying on his deckchair stiff as a corpse. He had on his massive signature glasses, so I couldn't read his expression. He was probably scouting for some talent. The guy had needs that I'm sure he wanted to fill while he was down here.

"When are you seeing him next?" Cassius asked, tucking into his food.

I stole a fry from his plate and answered, "He gets off at four."

Spencer chimed in. "I think Cass meant when are you seeing him, not blowing him."

"Ooh, look at you go, Spencey baby!" I whooped, raising my hands into the air. "A year of being one of us and you're becoming quite the shady lady."

"One of the advantages of being gay, right?" Spencer joked.

"Just don't harumpghkhjois."

"Uh, Cass, you might want to finish chewing first," I suggested.

Cassius chowed down the mouthful of food he'd inhaled and repeated more clearly this time. "Just don't outgay the OG gay, okay, baby?"

We all laughed, me the hardest. "Oh, Cass, sweetie. You're the worst gay in the world."

More laughter erupted from our area. Well, Cass, Spencer and I were laughing. Hawk wasn't. Wow, I guess I underestimated how horny he was. He was glaring straight ahead, in full-on hungry-for-ass mode.

Oh, well. Each to their own. The boys were here to have a fun weekend together, Hawk was on a mission for hole, and I had my sights set on the sexiest head of housekeeping known to humankind.

32

MIGUEL

I'd been keeping an eye out for Emry all day, but since we were back to full crew, I only emerged once from my office to grab a quick bite to eat. The rest of the day was spent in spreadsheet purgatory as I worked through more roster conflicts for the coming month, while looking over budgets for Leo who was curious to see whether we could reduce cleaning supply costs. Ri-ve-ting stuff, right?

Somehow, the day managed to go by relatively fast and at four on the dot, Emry was waiting for me in the lobby. He had his back to me as I approached him, and the way the light streamed in through the massive windows, he had an angelic aura about him. A funky looking angel that rocked a pink kaftan.

I smiled and took a moment to appreciate the fact that he'd flown all the way down here—for me!—before I gently tapped him on the shoulder. He spun around and practically flew into my arms and crashed his lips into mine. Clearly, he had no problems with public displays of affection...which yes, I probably should've figured out after he'd fucked me on my rooftop.

"I'm so happy you're here," I somehow wrangled out as Emry's kiss showed no sign of subsiding. After a few more wonderful moments, he finally pulled back, his hazel eyes shimmering with happiness.

"Me, too."

"Wanna go for a walk on the beach?" I suggested.

"Sure."

Emry slipped his hand into mine and that's how we walked through the resort and out onto the beach. I couldn't explain why, but a part of me was so proud to be walking next to him like this. Him in his pink kaftan, me in my all-black work uniform.

We stayed connected physically, but neither one of us said anything. I was dying to know what he was thinking, feeling. Was it all just me? Obsessing over him in a one-sided thing? I didn't even know what to call it. *Thing* was the wrong word, but right now, I couldn't find a better one.

I decided to bite the bullet as we made our way over the soft sand toward the water. "So, Emry, what's going on here?"

"Well, see that thing in the sky over there," he tipped his head toward the sun, "it's doing something called setting. It happens every day and—"

I pressed my index finger against his lips, interrupting Emry's obvious attempt of sidestepping my question with some lighthearted banter. "I mean, between us."

As I pulled away from him, his eyes glowed, reflecting the setting sun. The sheer radiance of his beauty sped my heart up to levels I was pretty sure weren't safe for the supporting of human life.

I shuffled my toes, digging them deeper into the still-warm sand. "Look, I know you probably have mixed feelings about me."

"I don't."

"Oh, okay. Maybe you're still hanging on to some residual hatred or resentment, which you're completely entitled to. I wouldn't blame you one bit."

"Nope. None of that, either."

"Huh?"

Emry hooked his fingers under my jaw and our eyes met, sending a rush of sweet tingles through my body. "I don't have any mixed feelings, Miguel. Like I told you last time we were together, I like you and...and I want to be with you." He carded his fingers through my hair. "What I want to know is—how do you feel? Do you have mixed feelings? Are you carrying around baggage from the past?"

Shit. Was I? That could explain why I'd been shifting from feeling numb to disconnected to over-the-moon happy over these past few weeks. "Maybe I am a bit, yeah," I replied meekly, shame flooding my gut. "I don't want to be trapped by the past anymore, but it's one thing to say it. It's another thing entirely to actually do it. It's hard."

Emry delicately cupped the sides of my face. "If we're going to have a future, Miguel, and I really hope we are, then you need to get over the past. Stop holding yourself hostage to what happened back then. Free yourself from it so that you can be here with me now."

It wasn't until Emry wiped the warm streak that fell down my cheek that I realized I'd started crying. I curled myself into him as years of shame, guilt, and regret poured out of me. He didn't say anything, but his hand rubbing up and down my back felt like all the relief I needed.

When my sobs lessened to just ugly-snort-crying, I pulled back and noticed the saturated patch on his kaftan. "Oh god, I'm so sorry. I've ruined it."

He looked down and smiled. "Don't worry. It doesn't matter, Miguel." His smile thinned when he spoke again. "I forgive you, Miguel. Yes, high school sucked and it was shit to get bullied. But it's done. It's not who we are anymore. And in a way, that horrible time has helped me to become the person I am today. Strong. Independent. Successful."

I chuckled. "And beautiful. And amazing. And wonderful." I was pretty sure those words were all kinda saying the same thing, but it was the best I had left in me.

Something was happening here. As the sun dipped lower toward the horizon line, I felt...lighter. Hearing Emry say he forgave me was the release I didn't know I had been waiting for, had been needing.

But as good as it was, it was only one side of the coin.

The other side was me finding a way to forgive myself.

He was right. I'd been holding myself hostage. But there was no way in hell I'd keep doing that if it meant missing out on the incredible gift that was standing before me.

Emry was way too good to give up.

33

EMRY

Was it wrong to admit that I was enjoying this beach walk with Miguel, even as I was pop-psychologizing my way through our conversation? I probably came across as either a lunatic or a much younger and hotter Dr. Phil substitute, but whatever. It seemed to be working.

I got the sense that Miguel's tears were long overdue. I was clear in my head that I wasn't giving him a pass by saying that I forgave him. There came a point where I had dealt with everything that had happened to me. In my own way. In a way that worked for me.

Miguel hadn't done that.

Years later, he was punishing himself like what he'd done in high school had happened yesterday. I hoped he had learned and grown from the experience, but from my vantage point, it looked like he was drowning in guilt and bad feelings, which, ironically, wouldn't help him grow at all.

We resumed our stroll, a delicate chill in the water nipping at our feet. "You know, you don't have to hold on to the past or anything that hurts you. It's okay to learn, grow, and look ahead."

Miguel nodded, releasing the last of his sniffles. His eyes were bleary and the tip of his nose was a rosy red, yet he looked just as adorable as ever. Maybe even more than normal because he was finally letting me in and showing me his vulnerable side.

"So, when you look ahead, Emry, what do you see?"

The sun hit his dark eyes, but all it illuminated was the pain that he'd held on to so tightly for all of these years. "I mean, about us," he clarified.

"I've been doing a lot of thinking," I began, which was an understatement. I'd been puzzling over this nonstop, weighing up all the different options and possibilities, trying to find a way to align my hopes with the reality we faced.

I stopped walking, took his hands into mine, and with a sharp inhale, uttered the scariest words that had ever come out of my mouth. "I'm falling for you, Miguel."

The relief that broke across his face vanquished all of the darkness in one breathless hit. He smiled so wide that it threatened to overtake the lower half of his face. His eyes sparkled as he pulled me in for a hug. "I'm falling for you, too, Emry," he whispered into my ear. "So fucking much."

As we pulled away, a figure standing in the distance caught my eye. Even from a few hundred feet away, I could feel Hawk's glare burning into me. Looked like my days of pop-psychologizing weren't over just yet. There was one more person in need of some of my Dr. Phil-ing attention.

34

MIGUEL

"You still here?"

I startled at Leo's voice coming from behind me. I spun around to face him, his impressive frame silhouetting the entire doorway.

"Uh-huh. I didn't get a chance to pack up when I finished at four."

A knowing smirk filled Leo's face. "Oh, yeah. Any particular reason for your rush to knock off?" he asked, pure teasing in his tone.

He knew I'd gone for a walk with Emry. I may have mentioned it...a few hundred times during the course of the day. What could I say? I was excited to see the guy.

"I don't mean to pry"—Leo walked over to the empty chair—"but I will." He let out a playful chuckle and his eyes sparkled with incandescent delight. I'd never seen this side to him before. To be fair, I'd never had someone I was interested in that he could needle me about.

Responding to my raised eyebrows, he lifted his palms to the side of his face. "What can I say? I'm a sucker for a good love story. And this is shaping up as one helluva good romance. Two small-town boys, from the same small town, go out into the world only to bump into each other here."

He was skipping over a lot of the details, but it didn't stop me from shaking my head and smiling as I continued gathering up my things and placing them into my satchel. "We went for a walk on the beach and it was...necessary."

"Necessary?" Leo looked like he'd swallowed a lemon.

"Yeah." I put my laptop into the bag before chewing the inside of my cheek. I'd told Leo about how Emry and I knew each other, sparing no details of how atrocious my behavior had been toward him. To my very pleasant surprise, Leo reserved all judgment, or if he did think less of me, he certainly did a good job of hiding it.

"I broke down and cried," I admitted, sitting down next to Leo.

"Hey, it takes a strong man to do that."

I smiled, loving that that was his immediate response.

"It's true, Miguel," he continued, focusing on me with soft yet serious eyes. "Owning your feelings and being able to express them, in whatever way they come out, is the true mark of a man."

"I know. It actually felt kinda good to get it out of me. I feel...lighter. Is that totally lame?"

His warm smile gave me the answer we both knew he didn't need to say.

"I have faith that you guys will be able to navigate this and find something that works for you both."

I bit down into my lower lip. "You do?"

Leo gave a calm nod. "Don't get me wrong, I'm not saying I'm a psychic and can predict the future here. But," he pointed his index finger at me, "I've seen enough guys fall in love around this place that I've developed a pretty good sense for how these things tend to pan out."

"But..." I stopped myself, not knowing how to phrase the enormity of what I wanted to say.

"But what?" Leo gently persisted after my silence stretched for longer than I'd intended.

"Life. Reality. Things." I hoped my wild hand gesturing compensated for not being able to string a sentence together. "He lives in Philadelphia. I live here. This is my job, and I love my job. His work takes him all over the world. We don't know each other that well. It's too early, too unrealistic for one of us to pack up our lives for the other. There's just so many *things*, Leo."

Leo's reassuring hand landed on my shoulder. "Life has a way of working things out, Miguel. Trust me on that one."

I looked him square in the eye. Leo had a decade and a half on me, so his words carried weight behind them. There was also something about the way he was looking at me. It was like he really believed what he was saying. It gave me a feeling I realized I'd never felt before: hope.

"Have you heard anything about the audition?" Leo asked, changing the subject.

I shook my head. "Nope. Which probably means I didn't get accepted."

"Or no news is good news," Leo countered.

I liked Leo's brand of optimism. It wasn't sickly sweet, but it was nice enough to always leave me feeling a bit better. As I took him in, I couldn't help but wish he'd find some of the happiness he was always helping everyone else achieve.

He said he liked being single and had a good life, but I knew that was only a half truth at best. His partner, Dante, was killed at least five years ago now, and Leo still wasn't totally over it. He never talked about it, though, and I never broached the topic. Still, I sent some positive love vibes his way.

"So, what's the plan, then?" Leo got to his feet.

I joined him, gathering the rest of my things as we headed to the door. "Emry's in his suite packing a few things and then we're going back to my place."

"So now you're poaching my customers, eh?" Leo quipped.

"What? No. Shit, sorry. Is that not allowed? I mean, they've paid for their room—"

"Miguel, relax. I was kidding. I'm trying to be funny."

I jammed my hands into my pockets. "Clearly a topic I know very little about."

"Hey, things will work out, Miguel. With Emry. About the audition. Just you wait and see. Sometimes, you gotta let go and just trust in life."

I blew out a heavy breath as I closed the office door behind us. "Just 'trust in life,' hey?"

All right. Let's see how that goes, shall we?

35

EMRY

"You're spending the night with him?"

The accusatory inflection in Hawk's voice made it sound like I had committed some horrible crime, like wearing bell bottoms unironically.

"That's right," I replied, continuing to pack up my stuff and not giving him the satisfaction of looking at him. "Oh, and *he* has a name, by the way."

"Whatever," Hawk snarled, and that was it, the tipping point that pushed me over the edge.

I stuffed the rest of my overnight essentials into my bag—just a few to-die-for vintage pieces I had picked up when I was in New York, along with some gorgeous bamboo sleepwear and toiletries— and marched over to the other side of the room. Hawk was perched at the edge of his bed, but I managed to get right up in his face. I peered down at him and growled, "What the hell is going on, Hawk?"

"Nothing," he said dismissively, brushing past me as he got up.

"No way." I latched onto his giant arm, and the momentum spun us both around so we were standing face to face, massive chest to my less-impressive chest. Hawk was sulking. Actually sulking. Yep. Arms folded across his chest, face as sour as a donkey's ass.

"No way what?" He glared at me and his jaw was doing that pissed-off ticking thing I'd seen it do a hundred times before, but this was the first time it was directed at me.

"We are not doing this stupid, shitty guy thing where we don't talk about what's going on," I shot back with the perfect combination of determination, *pissed-off-ness*, and a little sauciness to boot.

Hawk pulled back, but his eyes remained stuck to me. I knew him well enough to know what to do next. It was time to down the darkness and up the light. I had to soften the mood, crack a few silly jokes. It was the best way to get him to lower his defenses and tell me—once and for freaking all—what his real problem with Miguel was.

I began my comedic tirade with an overly dramatic hair flip. "This isn't a '90s rom-com, Hawk, and I am not, repeat not, Julia Roberts." I strutted over to the mirror and gave myself an approving once over as I took my reflection in. "But if it were," I twisted around to face him, an impish smile falling on my face, "I'd be more of a peak '90s Cameron Diaz. Don't you think?"

My silliness was having the desired effect as the first signs of a smile emerged, even though he was doing his best to fight it. His arms also went floppy, dangling by the side of his body without purpose.

"Ooh, actually, that's a really good Halloween costume idea," I declared with a sassy finger snap (yes, finger snaps can be made sassily, thank you).

"What is?" Hawk crinkled his face in confusion.

"Peak '90s Cameron Diaz...with an Emry Black slutty twist, of course."

Hawk's lips found that confused place somewhere between a smile and a smirk, unable to make a decision where to settle.

I wasn't done with him yet. I wanted a laugh. Okay, I'd settle for a chortle, but fun mouth sounds were the name of this little game. "But that's beside the point." I clapped my hands together before my eyes widened. "Actually, I want a do-over on that last sentence."

Hawk's lips were now stretched so wide he had no choice but to cover them with his hand to conceal them from my smug-ass self.

I cleared my throat and summoned the posh British accent gods to come through for me as I stated as regally as I could, "That's neither heaaarrr nor theaaarrre." I adjusted my posture from its regal tightness and slumped my way over to Hawk. The big guy was giggling behind his hand now.

Mission accomplished.

"There we go." I stepped in and pried his hands from his mouth. "Happy Hawk. That's how I like to see my friend."

As we faced each other, I held on to his hands and put as much gentleness into my voice as I could. "Something is definitely up here, Hawk. I know you don't like Miguel, and I'm pretty sure I know the reason why."

"You do?" The words squeaked out of his mouth in such a high pitch even a chipmunk would've heard them, scrunched up its cute little nose and gone, "Damn, girl, that's high."

Hawk cleared his throat and tried again. "You do?"

I nodded as I noticed our hand grip had changed. He was now holding on to my hands. "Yes. You're being a good friend. You're looking out for me and I appreciate it, Hawk. I really do."

His fingers squeezed mine tighter as a funny expression I'd never seen on him before crossed his face. "Actually, Emry, there's a little more to it than just a friend looking out for a friend."

"Oh?"

"You really want me to be honest with you?"

"Yeah, of course. You know you can tell me anything."

"Okay. Well, here it goes." Hawk's suddenly very clammy fingers wrapped even tighter around my hands as he closed his eyes and blurted out, "Emry...I think I'm in love with you."

Hawk's words hung thick in the air. It's fair to say I was blown away—and not in an *Oh my God, Taylor's just dropped a surprise album* kinda way. Call me blind and stupid, but I didn't see this one coming at all.

"How..." I stopped, not knowing what I wanted to ask Hawk. My friend. Finally, I managed to get a whole question out. "How do you know that you love me?" Gah, it was awkward and messy and I didn't even really know what I was getting at, but it was a starting point.

Hawk scratched the side of his face. "Brock."

My eyebrows pinched in tightly. "Brock?"

"Yeah. He's a guy we dick-twinned a while ago."

"Right. I remember. Brock the Jock."

Hawk half smiled. "That's the one."

"I'm not sure I follow though."

"I saw you come. I stared at your face while you came, Emry, and some people get ugly when they come. Their face twists and they're sweaty and totally lost in the moment. It's all good, it's just that, in that moment...you—you were beautiful."

"Oh." I didn't know what else to say.

"That's when it struck me. I've had the privilege of seeing you in that raw, intimate moment a number of times and it did something to me. It pulled me on the inside in some really fucking sappy way and that's why..." Hawk let out a long breath before he finished what he was saying. "That's why I think I'm in love with you, Emry."

I was touched by his sentiment and to hear Hawk talk like this. Believe me, no one knows better than me how rare it is for the guy to open up like this, to be so vulnerable.

I tread super carefully. "We have shared something amazing, Hawk. I have loved being dick twins. It's been wild and fun and just, the best thing ever. I don't regret it for a second. But what you're feeling, can I ask, is it love for me...or a desire for having what we've shared, with someone you can call your own?"

He clamped down on his bottom lip. After a few minutes passed, his face tightened. "Shit. I'm an idiot. And now, dammit, I've possibly fucked things up with you."

"No." My voice was firm. "You are not an idiot and you haven't fucked anything up, Hawk. I love you as a friend. And I always will."

"I love you as a friend, too, Emry."

We hugged and it was warm and deep and long. I meant what I'd said. Hawk hadn't fucked anything up. If anything, part of me knew that this would only make our friendship stronger. Why? Because we talked and we got the thing that was bothering Hawk, out of him, and into the open.

And *that* was the mark of a true friendship.

36

MIGUEL

Not a single peep.

Emry was so quiet on the ride over to my place, I was surprised we couldn't hear each other's blinks in my car. Something was on his mind; his demeanor had done a total one-eighty since our walk on the beach.

He seemed a little down, lost in his own head. I felt bad for thinking it, but whatever it was, I hoped it wasn't about me...or us.

Us.

Was there even an *us?*

Emry's words to me at the beach joined what Leo had said and it ricocheted around in my head. Emry's forgiveness made me start to look at things differently. Maybe it was finally time for me to leave the past...in the past.

It was only when I thought about letting all of the stuff that had happened, the things I had done to him go, that it dawned on me how tightly I'd been holding on to it. It was a coil I kept tightly wound around myself.

And Emry had been right. Keeping myself chained to a punishment spiral wasn't helping me grow or be a better person. Since time machines weren't a thing, and I couldn't erase what I'd done, and I'd pretty much exhausted the self-punishment option, the best thing I could do from now on was to apply the learnings from the lessons my mistakes had taught me.

Thoughts of letting the past go still whirred in my brain as I pulled into an empty parking spot in front of my building. Once we got into my apartment and Emry dropped his bag on the floor, that's when he broke the silence. "Hawk told me he's in love with me."

"Oh." I gestured to the couch and we sat down, doing my best to ignore the shiver that raced up my spine. "And are you in love with him?" I could feel my heart ticking in my ears. Shit. *This* was what had gotten him so tense. I suspected there was something more to them and now it looked like—

"No."

There was a steely determination behind his hazel eyes, but I wanted to know for certain. So, I pressed, "Are you sure, Emry? It's...it's okay if you are."

"I'm sure."

"How do you know?"

"Because." He dropped his head and let out a heavy breath. When he met my eyes again, the corners had softened, making him look even younger. "Because I'm falling in love with someone else."

Please say me. Please say me. "Who?" I choked out.

"You, you dweeb."

He threw a pillow at me. I didn't bother deflecting it. My reflexes, my body, my heart—everything was suspended by a wave of euphoria that had eluded me my whole life.

He patted the couch next to his leg and I scooted over, nestling into his side, desperate to get as close to him as I could.

"It's funny," Emry said wistfully as he threaded his fingers absently through my hair. "I've spent my whole adult life trying to get as far away as possible from my past, only to end up falling in love with someone from it."

"That's about as funny as my routine," I deadpanned, and his lips lifted.

His hand reached to the back of my neck and he pulled me in until our foreheads swayed into each other. "But where does it say that love has to make any sense?"

I scratched the side of my face. "Good question."

"I have no clue how this is going to work, but I do know one thing, Miguel."

"What?"

"One way or another, we *will* make it work."

I didn't doubt his conviction for one second, and the fierce kiss he planted on my lips confirmed it beyond a doubt.

37

EMRY

I was on a roll and feeling on top of the world.

It could have had something to do with the fact that I was exploring Miguel's mouth like I had just discovered a brand new continent. Because in some ways, that's exactly what it felt like.

His soft, surprised moan in response to my forceful entry into his mouth only turned me on even more. I straddled him, my knees burrowing into the couch as I dragged my fingers through his hair and drove my tongue deeper into him. My feelings for Miguel were strong and undeniable, and I wasn't going to pretend otherwise for a moment longer.

Hawk's admission in our room earlier had come as a complete surprise to me. I guess I'd been so caught up in what was unfolding with me and Miguel that I had mistaken his signs of jealousy as hints of protectiveness.

But we talked it out, like, you know, adults. Crazy, right?

We cared deeply for each other. There was no denying that. And Hawk was a great guy, a total catch. But we'd been blurring the lines between being good friends and dick twins for a while now. Perhaps, for a bit too long. While I'd never regret or feel even a snippet of shame for the fun we'd had together, it was time for that chapter of our friendship to come to an end. We both had needs that went beyond sex. Hawk wanted a connection with someone, and while he hadn't found the right guy yet, I knew that he would.

Meanwhile, I had my own list of naughty needs that I wanted met. And good thing Miguel was on the same page with me. I leaned in deeper to our kiss, allowing myself to feel the fullness of the lust and passion coursing through my body.

"I want to fuck you," I whimpered into Miguel's lips, the fierce need making me sound so unashamedly desperate.

Heat flared from Miguel as he pulled back slightly, his dark eyes aflame. "How? Soft or rough?"

I grazed his cheekbone with the back of my fingers. "However you want it, baby."

A smile lit up Miguel's entire face, like he was the happiest guy in the world. I felt the same. He leaned up and whispered into my ear, "How about soft, *then* rough?"

"Done."

We got to our feet and Miguel led me to his bedroom. The silence between us crackled with a different energy. Desire, yes, but something else, too. I guess it was the first time we'd be having sex after having opened up to each other about our feelings. That made it feel even more special.

We stripped out of our clothes and Miguel carefully laid himself down on the bed, looking at me with the most beautiful fuck-me eyes I'd ever seen.

"Someone's excited," he remarked, tipping his head toward my cock.

"Uh, you can talk," I shot back, pointing at his.

He let out a gentle laugh. "What are you doing standing all the way over there, Emry? The good stuff's right here."

I moved in closer. "Oh, is that so?"

He smirked. "Yeah."

The next thing I knew, he hooked his hands behind his knees and lifted his feet into the air. My breath caught in my throat at the sight of Miguel, lying on his back. Showing me all of him like that hit me. He looked so exposed, so vulnerable it made my knees buckle.

I crawled onto the bed, alternating between looking Miguel in the eyes and his beautiful, pink hole. Sure, we'd fucked twice, but I never got the chance to rim him. That was one of the most intimate things you could do with someone.

I brought the tip of my tongue to his sweet hole, inhaled his beautiful earthy scent, and then I made out with his ass, slurping, licking, and thrashing my tongue around. Miguel's body writhed under me and it felt incredible, knowing I was bringing him so much pleasure with just my tongue.

Suddenly, I stopped. "Wait."

He looked at me, his brow furrowed. "What is it?"

"You said you wanted soft, then rough."

"Changed my mind. Keep doing what you were doing. *Please*."

I smirked, in the mood to tease Miguel just a little more. "Are you sure, though? We made a plan and we really should stick to it."

"Plans are made to be broken," Miguel whined, wiggling his ass in front of me.

It was tempting, but I restrained myself for a moment longer, knowing that it would make the dive back in all the more sweet.

"You mean that?" I drawled. "Plans are made to be broken?"

"Yes. Yes. Yes." Miguel was practically panting at the moment. "Just get back down there. *Now*."

Was it wrong that the pleading in his voice was shooting jolts of desire straight to my cock?

"Beg me."

He looked down his body at me. "Huh?"

"If you want it, beg me for it."

A look of recognition, quickly followed by a fierce hunger, unleashed across Miguel's face as he let out a low, deep, "Please, Emry. Please eat my slutty hole."

"Slutty, eh?" I tapped my fingers against his wetness.

"For you," he moaned, his head tipped back in agony or ecstasy at my touch. I couldn't tell which. "Slutty for you. Only you."

"You mean it?"

"Promise. Cross my heart."

"Well, in that case..."

I hoped the windows in Miguel's apartment came with double glazing because the shout that roared out of him as I resumed tongue fucking him was the loudest sound I'd ever heard another person make. After I had driven him wild with my amazing tongue-lashing skills, I gave him what I knew he was craving.

When I entered him, his hips bucked against me and I gave him a moment to adjust his breathing and relax into it.

"Fuck me, Emry." His voice was dripping with need.

His words were all I needed to let go of everything I'd been holding on to my entire life—the pain, the fears, the loneliness—and in that moment, all I could feel was him. The warmth of him. The beauty of him.

I thrashed my hips into his body, slamming hard against him. "Oh fuck yeah," he cried out. "Harder."

I gave him exactly what he wanted, driving into his body with long, full movements. His eyes were closed and he was running his fingers through his hair. We were so connected with each other, yet he was also having his own experience of this as well.

I hoped that whatever was going on for him, it involved forgiveness and release. I pushed even deeper into him, hoping that I was reaching those parts of him that he held on to, that held him back. I wanted him to be happy. I wanted him to let go. I wanted us to have a proper shot at a happy future.

"Emry."

His voice stilled me instantly.

"Yes?"

"Can I—" His voice cracked, and I could see the vulnerability written all over his face. "Can I have soft now please?"

"Of course, baby." I lowered myself so that I could look into his soulful eyes. "You can have anything you want."

"Thank you."

With our bodies closer, I kissed Miguel while thrusting my hips, much more slowly this time. If I'd been giving him a hurricane experience before, this was more like waves gently rolling into the shore. It felt incredible for me.

"Does this feel good, Miguel?"

"So good," he moaned into my mouth.

We kept kissing, kept gently fucking for, like, a really long time. I'd never experienced this kind of pace before. My normal speed was frantic, balls to the wall, a hundred miles per hour. Going slow was my new favorite thing.

"I want to taste you," Miguel said, breaking our kiss.

"Uh, I think you already are," I teased.

"No, I mean...when you, uh, come."

"Oh, right. Okay... I want to taste you, too."

Miguel's eyes widened. "You do?"

"Of course. Are you ready now?"

Miguel gave a short nod, his lips parted slightly, as if he was in shock or something.

I peeled the condom off and assumed a sixty-nine position over Miguel's body, giving both of us perfect access to each other's cocks.

"You all good?" I asked.

No response—well, a muffled one. Miguel already had my cock stuffed down his throat.

This was going to be good!

38

MIGUEL

I began slurping away at Emry's exquisite shaft. God, it felt so dirty —in the best way possible—knowing he'd just been fucking me with it, and now it was in my mouth.

Something was happening here. I mean, yes, Emry was sucking my cock like a total boss and I hoped I was able to match him with my own efforts, but I didn't mean that. Something was lifting inside of me and it allowed me to be...free. Long-held thoughts and beliefs were being rearranged...I could feel it as strongly as I could his mouth slurping up my dick.

The freeing sensation allowed me to really enjoy the beauty of this moment and the incredible man I was with. For the first time in my life, I felt like it was okay to ask for what I wanted, knowing that it wouldn't be met with judgment or ridicule.

Emry was giving me everything I had always wanted, and I was ready to step up and give him everything he wanted, too.

I pulled his cock out of my mouth and groaned urgently, "I'm getting close."

"Come for me," he whispered back.

Emry swallowed me, before wrapping his fingers around the base, rotating his wrist in a way that set me off. After a few strokes, I rocked my hips and unleashed in his mouth. "Oh, oh...man, that's good," I cried.

I grabbed Emry's cock and filled my mouth with it, sucking it with all the urgency I could muster. I felt Emry's body shudder before his release filled me up.

Emry spun around and pulled up by my left side, propping himself up on his elbow. He traced his index finger along my jaw, back and forth in a soothing motion.

"How are you feeling?" he asked softly.

"Good."

He shot me an expectant look. So, I continued. "Scared. Happy. Free. Excited. And...hopeful."

"Hopeful?" His fingers were now playing with my earlobe.

"Yeah. Like maybe, somehow, this might be able to work."

"This will work, Miguel. I promise you. We've got some stuff to figure out, and both of us have a few things we need to work on, but I am confident we can do it. Together."

"Together." I repeated the word as a warm feeling blanketed my body. Oh, wait, no, that was Emry actually covering me with a blanket.

"Thank you."

He smiled but said nothing as he lay down next to me. We stared at the ceiling in silence for a while, letting everything catch up to us. I felt like I was on the verge of a brand new chapter in my life, one that wasn't written yet, one that we'd be filling out as we took our next steps, side by side.

I reached for his hand and interlaced our fingers. I could feel it bubbling inside me. I had to do it, no, I *wanted* to do it. It was scary and maybe too soon, but hey, sometimes, it's best not to make plans and just trust in life, right?

"Hey, Emry."

His eyes sparkled as he looked at me. "Yeah?"

"I love you."

He smiled as he breathed into me. "I love you, too, Miguel."

EPILOGUE - EMRY

SIX MONTHS LATER...

You could run to the ends of the earth, as far away as you possibly could from whatever it was you're escaping from...or at least, you could try.

As I'd been finding out every day for the past six months, sometimes it's good to let the past catch up to you.

Reconnecting with Miguel was as rare as getting struck by lightning...and proved to be just as amazing. After my last visit to Elysian, so much remained up in the air between us. But life finally conspired for us instead of against us, and bit by bit, the pieces of our puzzle came together.

It started with a phone call Miguel received the day after I'd left. He scored the gig with The Mean Comics. The second best bit? While they'd been impressed with his stand-up routine, they actually preferred his material over his delivery. They had an opening for a writer for their first-ever scripted series, and that's what they offered to Miguel. He was over the moon.

The best part? They were based in Philly, which meant we finally lived in the same state. Same zip code. Okay, same apartment. It started off as a temporary arrangement until Miguel got on his feet and made sure this was what he wanted, but somehow, he just never got around to finding his own place. You'd never hear me complaining about that.

In fact, these days, you wouldn't hear me complaining about anything, really. I went back to therapy. Not because I had a burning need to, and there was definitely no pressure from Miguel either. It was something I felt I wanted to do for myself.

Just because I'd had a bad experience with one therapist didn't mean there wasn't any benefit to therapy at all. I found myself a therapist who was a voracious LGBTQIA+ ally, and she was ah-ma-zing. She didn't want to simply rehash my past and blame my parents and family for everything. She took what was called a strengths-based approach. That meant that rather than trying to tear me down to build me back up again, she helped me channel my own innate fierceness and fill in any little cracks to help make me even stronger and better.

Our weekly Wednesday afternoon sessions had become something I actually looked forward to. I felt like I understood myself even better now. I saw that I had built up a fortress around my heart and that, in the same way that Miguel was chained to his past, it was keeping me tied to something I didn't want, too.

And as I was discovering, when you let your walls down, you let love in. And love was, like, the best thing in the whole world. Obviously, the true love between Miguel and me was incredible, but I'd recently stumbled upon another type of love: brotherly love.

Shortly after New Year's, I randomly got a text from an unknown number. It was Will. Turns out my older brother noticed my crumpled up Christmas card in the trash during the holidays and decided to get in touch with me.

We'd only exchanged a few messages so far. Kinda hard to catch up on so many lost years via text. He said he was doing well, was between jobs but okay about it, and had recently moved to Florida. He hinted at some "big changes" that had taken place in his life, but I had no clue what that meant or whether it referred to him or our parents. I hadn't heard diddly-squat from either of them, so at least some things stayed the same. I didn't know if Will would be open to meeting me, but I was working on getting the courage to ask him soon.

And Hawk? Well, my friendship with him had gone from strength to strength since we'd said goodbye to our legendary dick twin days. It was the end of an era but the start of an even better chapter of our lives.

He saw how happy Miguel made me, and after spending time with us and getting to know Miguel properly—free from the filters of the past and that godawful comedy routine—he didn't need me or Leo in his ear to sell him on Miguel's goodness and decency. He witnessed it with his very own eyes, and he'd come around.

That explained why he and Miguel were chatting and laughing away with each other, while I tried to get my tan on by the pool at Elysian. It was our first time back here with Miguel and me as boyfriends, and it felt...wonderful.

"You boys look like you're having fun." Leo's deep voice interrupted my daydreaming.

We took turns hugging the guy.

"Join us?" Hawk offered.

"I'd love to, but I'm dealing with a few issues at the moment. I just wanted to see you guys and say hi."

Miguel's jaw tightened. "Anything I can do to help?"

Leo let out a light chuckle. "Do I need to remind you that you no longer work here?"

Miguel lifted a brow. "I still can make up a mean bed and scrub a toilet down like it's never been scrubbed before."

"Truth," I added, raising both arms into the air. "You should see our bathroom back home. You could actually eat off any surface— it's that clean."

The guys chuckled. "Besides," Miguel added. "I'm sure I can still fit into that old uniform."

"Thank you, I appreciate the offer, Miguel," Leo said warmly as he gestured back toward the main office. "I should get going. We're dealing with a social media influencer who isn't happy about anything."

A chorus of groans escaped us. After another round of quick hugs, Leo left and Hawk got to his feet, too.

"And where do you think you're going, Mister?" I teased.

"Four o'clock," Hawk replied with all the seriousness of a drill sergeant. "There's a piece of ass over there that's calling my name."

"The poetry of it," Miguel observed, and we giggled.

"Hey." Hawk lifted a finger at us, a smile dancing on his lips. "Unlike some people here, I don't have sex on tap, so when the opportunity strikes, I need to take it. I'm horny and on the verge of dying of a case of the world's worst blue balls ever."

"Well, go ahead then," I said, waving him away. "Strike and be merry."

And with that, Hawk turned on his heel, leaving me to enjoy some quality time with my beautiful boyfriend.

EPILOGUE - MIGUEL

As much as Elysian would always hold a special place in my heart, it felt weird being back here. Why? Because I wasn't used to being here as a guest and doing typical guest-y things—like poolside hangs. It was taking me a moment to adjust and relax into the situation.

As Hawk trudged off in hot pursuit of his latest target, I threaded my fingers through Emry's. I exhaled, letting the warm sun beat down on me. I stretched my legs out, letting my feet dangle off the edge of the lounge chair as the sounds of laughter chirped around us.

"You good, baby?" Emry asked.

I glanced over at him lying beside me, wearing the fuck out of the skimpiest sequined pink G-string swimwear ever made. "I am," I sighed. "So, so happy. You look beautiful, by the way."

Emry ran his fingers cautiously along the top of his neck as a mild tremor overtook his lower lip. "Really?"

"Baby, makeup-free suits you."

I loved the fact that Emry wore makeup. As it turned out, he wasn't a fan. After about a month of living together, he admitted he only wore foundation to cover some of the nicks and remnants of his father's hands on his neck.

It made my blood boil to think what that man had done to him, and it made me sad that its effects still lingered. It took a lot for Emry to tell me about it. I just held him and listened without saying a thing, hoping my hand rubbing his back was soothing him in a way that no words would ever be able to.

At the end, I said these simple words, "You're most beautiful when you're happy."

I didn't mean anything by it other than stating the simple fact that whenever Emry laughed or smiled, that was when he truly shone the brightest. Over time, Emry began to apply less and less foundation until two weeks ago when he did something major: he performed without it.

That was a huge step for him, and I couldn't have been

prouder. There was no pressure from me at all. It was all him. I knew he was still a little self-conscious about it, so I made it my mission to pepper him with genuine compliments all day, every day.

A beautiful smile danced across Emry's face as he shuffled in his lounge chair, getting comfortable and tilting his head up to catch some rays. I couldn't help but smile, too, marveling at how much my life had changed over the last six months

I was finally pursuing my dream and I'd found the sweetest, most sacred kind of love I never even allowed myself to dream existed.

Working as a script writer at TMC was everything I wanted. It allowed me to go to some offensively mean comedic places while staying firmly *out* of the spotlight. I wasn't born to be the guy standing at the mic stand. I was meant to be the one writing the words that spilled out of his mouth.

Sure, I'd never become Seinfeld-level famous, but that was never my goal in the first place. My brain was weird and went to all sorts of uncharted places, finding a unique perspective on things that somehow, I was able to channel into a type of humor that appealed to some people. Being a writer on a show afforded me anonymity, while still doing the work I loved; that was the perfect mix of what I always wanted.

Besides, this relationship already had a shining star. I was wrong in thinking that falling in love with Emry Black would be the best thing to ever happen to me because *being* in love with Emry Black was even better.

I honestly wasn't expecting our living arrangement in Philly to be a permanent thing. No, really. I didn't want to rush things between us, so I fully expected to get settled, make sure I liked working on the show, and then find my own place near him. Hawk had offered for me to move in with him, and I seriously mulled it over for a while.

But then the most amazing thing happened. Emry and I fell

into this natural, free flowing groove living together, and as the days turned to weeks turned to months, moving out felt like the stupidest idea ever.

We just clicked, you know? Our natural rhythms gelled and we never fought over little things like leaving wet towels on the bathroom floor or whose turn it was to stack the dishwasher. Emry still traveled a lot, but that was okay. I used that time to put in some major hours with the writing team, so that when Emry was in town, I could work shorter days and spend more time with him.

When he was around, we settled into a routine that rotated around Netflix, finding cool new eateries in and around The Gayborhood, luxuriating couples massages at Emry's favorite day spa...oh, and sex. Lots and lots of rough, rugged, and soul-tender sex.

Being Emry's boyfriend was better than any dream I'd ever allowed myself to have. It left me wondering what other new and exciting and previously unthought of possibilities lay ahead of us. Marriage? Children?

Yes and yes. Not right now, of course, but in our future for sure.

But probably the biggest change I'd experienced since Emry and I got together was the one I felt within me. I thought I didn't deserve happiness, that torturing myself was the only path available to me for the mistakes I had made when I was younger.

Now I saw that there was another way forward. I'd stayed true to my word when I promised Emry that words were only the beginning. I now had a lifetime ahead of us to treat him with all the love, respect, kindness, and dignity that he deserved. And I knew in my heart of hearts that doing that would make me the happiest guy on the planet.

We still lived in a world that defined us using labels that were too narrow and restrictive. It also didn't allow us to change. What was once true of us in the past might not be who we wanted to be in the future.

Emry taught me a lot, including that being yourself was one of the bravest things you could do. But just as importantly, he made me see that even if I didn't have it all figured out, even if I screwed up and took more than a few wrong turns, I was still loveable and still deserved to be happy, just like everyone else.

And of all the things about Emry Black that I was grateful for, that might be the gift I cherished the most.

"Oh, hey." I tapped Emry on his shoulder. "Looks like Hawk's scored." I tipped my head to the right, just as Hawk sent us a friendly wave, holding the hand of a cute, dark blond otter, walking half a step behind him.

Emry shrieked, like the time he thought he'd seen a spider but it was really a moth.

"What's wrong?" I bolted upright, giving Emry my full attention.

Emry peeled the sunglasses off his face and squinted with intensity over at Hawk and the guy he'd picked up. His mouth was hanging so far open, I looked around to make sure no moths were around to fly into it.

"Baby?" I asked, starting to get a little worried. "What's wrong?"

"That guy Hawk's with," Emry gulped, turning to face me, his face drained of color. "That guy is...my brother."

THE END

ABOUT CASEY COX

Casey Cox is an Australian MM romance author who writes stories filled with love, laughter, and happily ever afters!

Casey loves spending time at the beach and is the proud paw-rent to two utterly adorable French Bulldogs - Ralphie and Lilly.

For more information about Casey, please visit -
www.caseycoxbooks.com

www.ingramcontent.com/pod-product-compliance
Lightning Source LLC
Chambersburg PA
CBHW020550020726
47494CB00006B/2000